'Mistress Isabel'—Sir F[...]
his steely hands—'tell [...]
meet in secret while yo[...]
I have a right to know[...]

'You have no right[...]
gance, Isabel lost her f[...]
a burning anger. 'You a[...]
betrothed, and I will never marry you. Let me g[...]
once. I wish to return to my bed.'

He released her and picked up the candle but,
just as she took a step forward, his free hand shot
out and pulled her cloak wide apart. Shocked into
immobility, she stood naked in front of him. He let
the cloak fall and, speechless with shame, she
clasped it tightly around her.

'So . . .' His voice was icy cold. 'Your lover holds
you tight in his arms, all yielding softness against his
manhood. Who is this fortunate young man who
has perhaps already stolen your maidenhood?'

Mary Bowring was born in Suffolk. She went to a convent school in Belgium, joined the Women's Auxiliary Air Force in the Second World War during which time she met and married her husband who was in the Army. She took up writing after the birth of a son and daughter and published three books about her life as a veterinary surgeon's wife.

The Phoenix Flame is her first Masquerade Historical Romance and is set in one of the most controversial and divisive periods in our history.

THE PHOENIX FLAME

MARY BOWRING

MILLS & BOON LIMITED
15–16 BROOK'S MEWS
LONDON W1A 1DR

First published in Great Britain 1985
by Mills & Boon Limited

© Mary Bowring 1985

Australian copyright 1985
Philippine copyright 1985
This edition 1985

ISBN 0 263 75099 X

Set in 11 on 11½ pt Linotron Times
04–0585–58,400

Photoset by Rowland Phototypesetting Ltd
Bury St Edmunds, Suffolk
Made and printed in Great Britain by
Cox & Wyman Ltd, Reading

CHAPTER
ONE

HOLSTEAD HALL lay sleeping in the hot sunshine of an August afternoon. The entire household within its timbered and plastered walls seemed to have succumbed to the heat of this summer of 1581 and only the drowsy cooing from the dovecot in the cobbled courtyard gave any indication of life.

Suddenly there was a flutter of wings, and the birds scattered as a side door opened and a girl ran quickly over to the stable yard. A few minutes later, mounted on a chestnut mare, she rode out and, with a quick glance up at the windows of the silent house, turned off into the woods at the side of the west lawn. Once out of sight, she slackened the reins and let the mare pick her way through the trees.

Momentarily she looked down and a slight frown marred the smoothness of her young forehead. She had changed hastily and this riding-habit was old and shabby. Then she shrugged lightly. There was no need to make herself splendid in order to visit Anthony, whom she had known since childhood.

How, she wondered, would he take the bad news she was bringing? Would he be able to advise her or would he tell her she must obey her parents as all dutiful daughters should? In spite of the hot afternoon a chill swept over her as she recalled her mother's words of the day before.

'You should be thankful,' Lady Holstead had said reprovingly, 'that your father has been released from the Tower, and grateful to the good friend who has secured his freedom. You are fortunate indeed to have the opportunity of marrying such a fine man. It will be a splendid match for you. Sir Ralph Overton is very rich.'

Such startling news, together with the calm assumption that the matter was already settled, had dismayed and alarmed Isabel. Always a little in awe of her stately though loving mother, she had tried nevertheless to express her fears, saying that she could hardly remember Sir Ralph, having seen him only once, and that was years ago. Then she had added desperately, 'I cannot even recall his face. I only remember that he was tall and haughty.'

Her mother had brushed this aside.

'He has remembered you well enough, you may be sure. His father and yours were boys together, and it was always their hope that, one day, their two families would be united by marriage. Sir John, as you know, died last year and now that his son has come into his inheritance he is anxious, no doubt, to fulfil his father's wish.' Lady Holstead's delicate face had lit up with a rare smile. 'Isabel, my darling, are you not glad that your dear father is coming home at last? Three months he has been in that dreadful Tower, and would be there still if Sir Ralph had not paid his fines.'

Of course she was glad, though she found it surprising that her father had allowed his fines to be paid for him. Last time, when he had had to sell some of his land to pay the Commission, he had said he would die rather than sell any more, and that they had no right to make an honest Catholic suffer for remaining faithful to his religion. She had reminded her mother of what Sir Nicholas had said, and Lady Holstead flushed indignantly.

'You must not question your father's decision. The Tower is a fearful place, and he has been in ill health ever since he was taken there. It may well be that Sir Ralph paid the fines without your father's leave. We shall know more tomorrow when they both arrive. I, for one, am so happy that I could weep for joy.'

It was then that Isabel had resolved to steal away next day and ask Anthony's help. At the thought of his comforting friendship her spirits rose and, tightening the reins as the mare stepped out of the wood, she urged her on over the last three miles of open country.

At the great door of Vale Court she hesitated for a moment. Should she announce herself and run the risk of encountering Anthony's father—that serious scholarly man who always spoke kindly to her, but seemed to be far away with his mind on his books? Much as she liked him and held him in esteem, she would rather see Anthony alone. Mr Norton was a widower and a devout Protestant, though this fact made no difference to the friendliness existing between the two families. Both he and Sir Nicholas were sincere in their opposing beliefs but wisely saw no reason why their friendship should be darkened by the intolerant practices adopted by the extremists on both sides. Anthony's father had suffered much anxiety in the reign of Queen Mary Tudor and had been obliged to take refuge abroad in Protestant countries with his young delicate wife, who had died far from her home. When, at last, the Princess Elizabeth had come to the throne, Mr Norton had returned with his baby son and settled down to a peaceful studious life with his books and his friendly neighbours.

Now it was the turn of Isabel's family to suffer and, because Sir Nicholas would not attend the Protestant service on Sundays in the parish church, he was classed as a recusant and obliged to pay large fines for refusing to conform. Gradually he was becoming impoverished and, sometimes, when Isabel saw her mother's tears, she grew fearful for the future.

But, at nineteen, it was difficult to be anxious for long, and Anthony helped to keep up her spirits. Things would become easier, one day, he told her. If the Queen were to marry a Catholic prince, as the rumours said, then there might be a compromise and folk would be allowed to worship as they chose.

Once more she was in need of comfort and, with the threat of marriage uppermost in her mind, went in search of Anthony. She found him, as she expected, round by the Mews where he was engrossed in petting his favourite goshawk. A tall young man of twenty-two with thick fair hair, he was handsome and strong, with a healthy complexion because of the hours he spent in the open air seeing to the affairs of his father's estate.

He turned and greeted her cheerfully, his smile reflected in his deep blue eyes.

'Isabel! We had great sport early this morning. Jezebel here excelled herself. We had a grand chase, though I lost my hat and fell into a bog-hole. Come and give her a kiss to praise her for her skill.'

Isabel drew back, smiling. 'I shall kiss your dog most willingly'—she bent down and patted the spaniel at his feet—'but Jezebel glares at me so furiously that my courage fails.'

Anthony laughed gently, then looked at her more closely. 'You are pale, and I see signs of recent tears.' He hesitated for a moment, then, as he saw her lips quiver at his sympathy, asked quickly, 'Your father—Have you news of him?'

Her face lit up. 'Oh, yes! Good news. He is coming home this evening. We are all overjoyed.'

'Why, then, I must have been mistaken. Your tears were those of happiness.' He paused, and added thoughtfully, 'Your father is a brave man. Perhaps he has found the solution to his troubles. Prison for a few months instead of having to pay those monstrous fines that can end only in ruin.'

Isabel shook her head. 'No, Anthony. He was released only because his fine was paid. A friend has rescued him this time.' She put her hand on his arm. 'Stay for a little while, before we go to your father. There is more to tell.'

'Ah!' His smile faded and, with a quick glance at her serious face, he led her over to a bench against the wall. 'Come, sit here in the shade. You know I have only one wish, and that is to serve you, my Isabel.'

She flushed at the warmth in his voice and, as he took her hand in his, gazed thoughtfully down at the sight of her own pale fingers being gently stroked by his brown, strong masculine ones. For a moment she forgot her troubles in the sweet peacefulness that engulfed her, and sat silent with a strange new sensation in her heart.

Lifting her head at last, she turned to look at him

and saw an expression in his eyes that she had never before encountered. Quickly she dropped her gaze and began to speak, hurriedly and almost incoherently.

Anthony listened in silence and tried to give her his full attention, but he too was distracted by the intensity of his feelings.

For some time he had been conscious that he loved Isabel. It had come to him one morning when he had met her riding towards his house with a message from her mother. Up till that moment the day had been dreary and cold, with the frosts and snow of winter turning into a grey wet spring. Then, as he caught sight of the chestnut mare cantering towards him and the slender rider waving joyously as she approached, the whole world suddenly seemed to be enveloped in a golden radiance. He knew then that Isabel was not only his dearest friend and confidante, but the only woman he would ever love.

This, he realised, was what his father had meant when, long ago, he had told him that he could never bring himself to provide a stepmother for his son. No other woman would ever replace the beautiful creature who had left him so desolate without her. Still stroking Isabel's soft hand, Anthony noticed at last that she was staring at him in astonishment.

'You have not, I swear, heard one word of what I have said. Do you think, perhaps, it is a small matter that I have to marry a man I can scarcely remember?'

She pulled her hand from under his and put it to her mouth to stifle a sob and, horrified, he took her roughly by the shoulders.

'Marriage? What talk is this?'

'Oh, Anthony!' Isabel smiled through her tears. 'I thought—well, no matter—your mind, no doubt, was on your falcons.'

His heart pounding, Anthony pulled her into his arms. 'No, my sweet. My mind was full of you. I was thinking that I love you. There! I have said it, and now . . .' Bending his head, he kissed her gently on the lips and then, feeling her soft willing response, held her so tightly that she could scarcely breathe.

Suddenly she wrenched herself free and, covering her face with her hands, broke into a passion of weeping.

Helplessly, his face grown pale, he watched her, not daring to touch her again until at last she dried her eyes and began her tale once more.

Finally she looked up at him despairingly. 'So, you see, I am caught. If this Sir Ralph is to continue helping my father . . .'

'Of that you cannot be certain,' Anthony said quickly. 'If you tell him that you love me . . .' He stopped. Perhaps he was assuming too much. 'Isabel,' he asked urgently, 'do you love me?'

He waited, his heart beating so fast he thought he would choke, until she nodded mutely and looked up at him, the answer written plainly in her eyes.

For a few minutes they sat in blissful silence then, suddenly, Isabel exclaimed, 'Our parents . . . Oh, Anthony! What will they say to us?'

'They will understand,' he said stoutly. 'My father and your father are good friends. They should rejoice that we love each other, even though . . .' Suddenly doubts swept over him as he began to see the difficulties that lay in their path. 'What if we are of different faiths?' he said desperately. 'If

the Queen can marry a Catholic, then why should
not I be allowed to follow her example?'

'The Queen plays with her suitors, my father
says. She will never take a Catholic husband. She
knows her people would turn against her, though
we Catholics are her subjects too,' Isabel added
with unusual bitterness, 'and just as loyal as the
Protestants, despite what her advisers say.'

'This Sir Ralph . . .' Anthony felt a furious surge
of jealousy. 'He is, I suppose, a Catholic—his
sympathy in your father's troubles is plain to see.
And he is rich, you say?'

She nodded miserably. 'Very rich. He has a large
estate in Kent—a great house there—and land in
the west country. He also has a house in London,
where my father spent last night before setting out
to come home.'

She looked at the deepening shadows in the
courtyard and said quickly, 'I must go. My father
will be arriving before sunset and I have to be
dressed in my fine gown to welcome him, though I
do not think he will see far beyond my mother.'

''Tis not for your father that you must be made
even more beautiful,' he said angrily. Then, as her
eyes darkened with fear, he added more gently,
'You came for help to me, and I have offered none.
But we have discovered our love for each other,
and that must be the armour we will wear for our
protection. Tonight I shall speak with my father,
and tomorrow we shall call to welcome Sir Nicholas
home and ask his blessing on our marriage. As for
Sir Ralph,' he looked at her appealingly, 'show him
no kindness, my sweet. He asks too high a price for
his generosity.'

'Show him no kindness'—the words kept repeating themselves in Isabel's head as she cantered across the fields, and she resolved to put them into practice, however hard it might be to risk her parents' disapproval. Filled with determination, refusing to think any further than the next day when her father would learn that there were two suitors for his daughter's hand, her spirits rose as she approached her home.

Now there was great activity everywhere. Servants were rushing about their business, there was a noise of clattering in the kitchen quarters and she was greeted excitedly by Will Rayner, the man who looked after the horses.

'Not long to wait, Mistress,' he said, his round face beaming with pleasure as he helped her to dismount. 'Your father should be here within the hour. Your lady mother is in the oak parlour, waiting to speak with you.' He hesitated and gave her a quick, compassionate grin. 'She sent word that you must go to her at once. She is very displeased that you have left so little time in which to prepare yourself for your father's arrival.'

Isabel smiled as she replied, 'An hour, you say? That is time enough for me, so long as my mother does not delay me with a lecture.'

'Hasten, then!' Will turned to lead the mare away. 'It would not do for you to spoil her joy on this great day. Indeed, we are all so eager to see Sir Nicholas again that we can scarcely keep our wits about us.'

She laughed and went quickly indoors to be greeted by smiling servants, but when she went into the oak parlour her mother, already magnificently dressed in a green and gold satin gown, received her coldly. 'You have been to Vale Court, I suppose. Had I known what was in your mind, I would not have let you go.'

Isabel stared. 'But, Mother, you have never before forbidden me to visit our friends.'

'You saw Mr Norton?'

She flushed guiltily. 'He was in the house, but I talked to Anthony in the Mews, and there was no time . . .' She stopped as she saw the stern disapproval on her mother's face. It seemed that her days of freedom were over. No longer would she be allowed to come and go as she pleased.

Lady Holstead's eyes grew kinder at the sight of her daughter's dismay. 'There, now. I shall say no more. But you must remember that you are a woman grown and being sought after in marriage. There must be no more of these solitary rides to Vale Court. Mr Norton and Anthony are our good friends and, I hope, will continue to be so, but you may not visit Anthony alone when you are betrothed to Sir Ralph Overton.'

'When?—Mother, why do you not say "if"? Sir Ralph may not be serious in offering for my hand— My father may have misunderstood his intentions. As for me, I know full well the answer I shall give him if he asks me to be his wife.'

'And that will be?'

'It must be No,' said Isabel calmly, though her heart was thumping in her breast and she found it hard to look her mother in the face.

'"Must?" What word is this?' Lady Holstead drew herself even more erect. 'There is only one "must" for a daughter. She must obey her parents, trust in her father's judgment and be dutiful. That is the only way to true happiness.' Her voice softened as she saw Isabel's lips tremble. 'We may talk no longer. The maids are waiting to help you to dress.'

Alice and Joan, red-faced with excitement, were chattering merrily as Isabel entered her bedchamber but, at the sight of their mistress's face, glanced quickly at each other and fell silent. When at last their task was done they stood, hands clasped, gazing at her in awed admiration.

Always beautiful with her pale skin and thick golden hair, Isabel's loveliness was doubly enhanced by the richness of her best gown. The tight ivory bodice emphasised her slim waist; then, spreading out over the farthingale, the skirt fell apart to reveal the delicately embroidered primrose silk underskirt. The oversleeves were short and puffed out at the top, and tight undersleeves of the same material as her kirtle ended in a tiny ruff at the wrists. Her hair shone through a caul made of gold thread decorated with pearls and worn at the back of her head, and a white ruff kept her neck erect.

'Oh, Mistress!' Alice, the elder girl, sighed dreamily. 'Sir Ralph will fall at your feet. You seem his bride already.'

'Bride?' Isabel's eyes flashed in sudden anger. 'What silly talk is this? I am dressed to welcome my father home. Sir Ralph is our guest, and that is all.' She turned to the younger girl. 'Joan, you may go now. I wish to speak with Alice.'

As the door closed, Isabel sighed. 'Alice—It seems that all the servants are talking of my future. You have been my friend since we were children together, and to you I can open my heart. What shall I do? I cannot marry this stranger who is coming with my father.'

Alice looked puzzled. 'If your father wishes it,

then you will have to obey. From what I hear, Sir Ralph is a great gentleman and a good Catholic. It will be a fine match for you. Ah! Do not weep—it will spoil your beauty.' She took Isabel's hand and held it tightly. 'It is indeed a sad thing to have to leave your home, and it is natural to be fearful, but see how happy your lady mother is with your father. Yet I have heard it said that when she came here, a bride of sixteen years, she wept for a whole week and would not be comforted.'

Isabel looked at her in amazement. 'You know more than I do, then,' she said slowly, 'but my case is different. I . . .' She stopped suddenly and turned away to prevent Alice from reading the truth in her tear-filled eyes. Not even to this faithful servant and friend could she confide her secret. It must be kept in her heart until Anthony's father had spoken with her parents. Forcing a smile, she turned towards the door.

'Do not look so anxious, Alice. Perhaps something may happen to change my father's mind. I must go down now, or my mother will scold.'

She had reached the bend in the staircase when she heard her mother's voice. 'Hasten! Hasten! Isabel, do you not hear the noise? Your father has arrived.'

Even as she spoke, the great door was flung open and, suddenly, there was Sir Nicholas standing below, his arms stretched wide to embrace her mother. Soon it was Isabel's turn, and the next few minutes were full of the joyous sounds of reunion.

At last Sir Nicholas, tears streaming down his face, stood back and shook his head as if bemused. 'I can scarce believe it, even now. There were times in that grim place when I thought I would never see you again. When I was ill of the fever and thought my last hour had come, the dream that helped me recover was this one—my beloved wife and daughter in my arms and I in my own home again.'

Isabel, drying her own tears, looked at her father searchingly. His sufferings had left their mark. A vigorous man of fifty with hazel eyes full of fire and vivacity had been taken, protesting violently, to the Tower, but a stranger had returned. His hair was grey, his face pale and thin, and his riding-clothes hung on him loosely.

'My love,' Lady Holstead said quietly, 'I shall nurse you well, so that soon you will be your old self. But first I must thank your benefactor. Sir Ralph'—she looked over to the door—'do not hide yourself from us! We owe you more than we can ever tell.'

Suddenly Isabel's heart began to pound, as she found herself staring at the tall man who came forward to kiss her mother's hand.

'My lady'—his voice was deep and rich—'it was a privilege to help my father's friend. We must keep together now. The times are hard for us, and likely to get harder.'

Lady Holstead nodded gravely and, as they talked, Isabel studied their guest.

He could not be more than eight-and-twenty, but he had an air of self-confidence and authority that spoke of power and great possessions. He wore his dark hair rather long, but his beard was neatly trimmed to a point. It was his deep-set eyes, however, that held her attention. Almost black and full of expression—kind, now as they looked at her mother—but capable, she felt sure, of fierce anger if he were thwarted.

Suddenly she found those same eyes fixed on her as her mother turned and, confused, she dropped a deep curtsy, feeling her face grow hot as she rose and saw his gaze sweep her from head to foot in one appraising glance.

'Mistress . . .' He bowed, but the servants came in with the baggage they had unloaded, as he began to speak, and she missed his opening words.

For a minute she stood tongue-tied, hypnotised by the unreadable expression in his eyes, then, to her great relief, her mother drew them all into the oak parlour.

'We shall have supper as soon as you have washed,' she said. 'But first you must take a measure of wine to refresh you after your long ride.' She turned to her guest. 'Sir Ralph, your bedchamber is prepared for you. The servants will show you the way, when you are ready.'

Carefully keeping in the background, Isabel sipped her wine slowly, her eyes fixed on her father. A few minutes later, Sir Ralph bowed and left the room.

Sir Nicholas looked at his wife. 'You have told our daughter?'

'Yes, my darling.' Lady Holstead glanced at Isabel, and saw that she had overheard the question.

'Well, then, my sweet child,' Sir Nicholas turned and smiled at her. 'Are you not pleased with your father? Ralph is a fine young man, a worthy son of my old friend. You, my Isabel, will make him a fit and beautiful wife. This is a great day for all of us . . .' He paused. 'You are happy, are you not?'

Isabel hesitated. This was the moment to make

her stand, but how could she take the joy out of her father's first hour of reunion? Her mother too was looking at her beseechingly—it could not be said just yet. She must choose a better time.

She smiled gravely. 'I am happy indeed, Father.' She put her hand in his. 'It is wonderful to have you back with us once more.'

Later, when they had eaten in the hall, they went up to Lady Holstead's withdrawing chamber on the first floor, a gracious room filled with feminine touches. Tapestries and portraits hung on the panelled walls and there was a wide window-ledge on which Isabel seated herself and turned to gaze out through the open window over the garden.

So far, she had managed to avoid speech with Sir Ralph, but soon she regretted having chosen the window-seat for, to her dismay, he left his place beside her father and came towards her, a smile hovering round his lips and that same inscrutable expression in his dark eyes.

'You spread your skirts wide, Mistress Isabel, but, even so, I think there is room and plenty for two. Will you permit me to share your refuge?'

Unable to refuse, and conscious of her mother's quick glance in her direction, she nodded coolly, and his smile grew broader as he seated himself beside her.

She had scarcely looked at him during supper, but now she could not help seeing how very grand he was since he had changed from his travelling clothes. His black velvet cloak was thrown back to reveal a rose-coloured doublet shot with gold. He wore a long heavy gold chain round his neck, a high-standing collar surrounded his white ruff, and his shoes were of the softest Italian leather.

Suddenly aware that he was amused at her scrutiny, she flushed, and turned quickly to look out of the window.

'Do I not merit a few words from you, Mistress?' His tone was slightly mocking. 'Or can it be that your beauty hides a tragedy, and that you are mute?'

Involuntarily she smiled. 'Far from it, sir. I owe you many words of thanks for securing my father's release. We—my mother and I—shall always be in your debt.'

'You must not think of it in that fashion,' he said gravely. 'Indeed,' laughing gently, 'I had a fierce struggle to obtain your father's permission to pay his fines. He would, I think, almost have preferred to stay in that miserable place, but that he was ill and longed for his home and family.'

Isabel looked at him coldly. 'Nevertheless, a debt must always be repaid. What favour do you ask, Sir Ralph?'

He frowned.

'There is, as I said, no question of repayment. Ah!'—he saw her eyes flash scornfully—'now I perceive your meaning. Your mother has spoken to you, and you have linked two things together. But you misjudge me. True, I have asked for your hand in marriage, but that has naught to do with payment of your father's fines. Our marriage was arranged for us by our parents when we were children. Did you not know?'

Horrified, Isabel stared at him, her eyes wide with dismay, and his frown deepened as he rose slowly to his feet. Then he turned to her parents at the far end of the room.

'Have I your permission, Sir Nicholas, to walk a

little in the gallery with Mistress Isabel? We have much to say to each other.'

Sir Nicholas nodded, glanced quickly at his wife, and smiled at his daughter. 'You must show Sir Ralph the portrait of his father,' he said jovially. 'It was painted when he and I were young together, and you will see how like the son is to his father—a fine man, and my best friend.'

There was nothing for it, and reluctantly Isabel stood up and led the way out of the room. But as soon as they entered the long gallery where the last rays of the sunset were flaming through the west window, she seated herself resolutely on a bench against the panelled wall.

'I have no wish to walk with you, Sir Ralph,' she said composedly. 'Let us get this matter settled quickly. I am honoured that you wish to marry me, but I must ask you to release me from a promise which you say our parents made on our behalf when we were too young to understand.'

Bracing herself, she prepared to face the storm and looked at him steadily but, unexpectedly, he was silent. For a full minute he returned her gaze, his eyebrows raised, then, his mouth twitching as though he were trying to control a smile, he turned away.

Puzzled and uncertain, she watched him stroll down the gallery until at last he stopped in front of the large portrait of their two fathers standing side by side with pet dogs at their feet.

'My father was right,' he said. 'He saw you when you were three years old and told my mother that you would be a great beauty, but wilful and hard to tame.'

He smiled down at her and, before she could

escape, pulled her to her feet and into his arms. 'But this, my sweet rebel, is how I shall tame you.'

She wanted to scream, to beat at his face with her fists but, helpless in that strong grip, she could only submit as his lips came down on hers. At last he released her and she leant against the wall, gasping for breath. Her eyes blazing with anger, she reached out to strike him, but he caught her hand and held it tightly.

'Come,' he said calmly, 'let us go to your parents and ask their blessing.'

CHAPTER
TWO

LATE THAT night when the house was quiet, Isabel lay wide awake. Tossing and turning, she relived the scene in the long gallery and remembered the relief she had felt when, on re-entering the withdrawing room, her mother had stopped Sir Ralph as he began to speak.

Pointing to her husband heavily asleep in his chair, she whispered, 'Sir Nicholas is not well. We must get him to his bed.'

Later Isabel went in to see her father and, although he had recovered a little and greeted her smilingly, she had been alarmed at his pallor and weakness. But that, he assured her, was of no consequence.

'All I need is a day's rest and I shall be up and about, for there is much I have to do. You will not go to your husband empty-handed, my sweet daughter. The lawyers must be consulted, and all things properly arranged.'

'But, Father . . .' Isabel stopped as Sir Nicholas closed his eyes, looking so exhausted that she dare not voice her protest. A minute later her mother, worried and preoccupied, entered and Isabel slipped away to her own room.

It seemed that the Fates were against her. Filled with foreboding, she lay in the darkness trying to find the words in which to explain matters to her parents without arousing their anger. At last, overwhelmed by the heat of the summer night, she climbed down from her bed and walked barefoot over the polished boards to the window. Flinging wide the shutters, she stood breathing in the sweet-scented air and tried to rid herself of the fears crowding in on her like a bad dream.

Leaning out of the open casement, she let the breeze play on her flushed face and it was then that she heard the quiet clip-clop of a horse's hooves. She stiffened, staring out over the moonlit garden and, suddenly catching her breath, saw the dark shape of a man ride out from the shadows, dismount, and tie his horse to a tree. Then, as he walked stealthily towards the house, her heart began to race. She leant further out of the window, waving wildly until he looked up and saw her.

'Anthony,' she called as loudly as she dared, and he pulled off his hat, staring at her as though he were seeing a vision.

At last she heard him whisper, 'Come down, Isabel. Come through the side door. I must speak with you.'

Hastily she turned back into the room, realising with a gasp of shame that she was naked, having thrown off her shift in her efforts to get cool. Pulling out the chest at the foot of her bed, she drew out a long cloak. To her dismay, the lid slipped from her nervous fingers and she stood in agony for a moment, praying that Alice, who slept in the little room through her own bedchamber, would not be awakened. But, just as she had decided that all was well, the girl appeared, rubbing her eyes sleepily.

'I heard something . . .' Suddenly wide awake, she stared at Isabel.

'Mistress—are you ill?'

'Hush! Go back to bed,' Isabel whispered. 'Anthony is below, and I am going to speak with him.'

'You cannot go alone!' Alice looked horrified. 'If you should be caught, it is better that I should be with you.'

Isabel hesitated, then nodded. 'Very well.' She bent down and opened the chest again. 'Wrap yourself in this and put on these slippers. Be quiet as a mouse, and follow me.'

A few minutes later, turning the key in the lock of the side door, Isabel said softly, 'Stay inside and keep guard. If you hear anything untoward, open the door and call me very quietly.'

Alice nodded obediently and Isabel stepped outside into the small courtyard.

The moon had disappeared behind a cloud, and all was hidden in darkness. For a moment her courage failed. She should not have come . . . If she were discovered . . . She shivered, and was about to turn back, when she heard her name. The whisper came from her left and, with a half-sob of relief, she found herself in Anthony's arms.

'Come this way,' he said, drawing her away from the doorway. 'We are too near the kitchen. There will be servants sleeping.'

In an alcove on the far side of the courtyard he stopped. Pulling back the hood covering her head, he buried his face in her hair for a moment, then said brokenly, 'My love, I have bad news. My father is against our marriage.'

The blood seemed to drain from her heart, and

she swayed and would have fallen, but he held her closely and went on hurriedly, 'I told him this evening after supper, never thinking but that he would be overjoyed at my choice. For a while he said nothing, then slowly he shook his head. It was impossible, he said. Such a thing could never be. Your parents, he knew, would never permit you to marry a Protestant, and he himself, though he pitied me from the depths of his heart, could not allow me to marry into a Catholic family. I tried! Oh, how I tried . . .' Anthony gave a sob of despair. 'I reminded him that he had loved one woman only and that I too had found my true love, but he stayed firm, insisting that the cases were not the same. He refused to mention the matter to your father because he said he knew only too well that his views would be the same.' He paused and buried his face once more in her hair; then, his voice muffled so that she could scarcely hear, he added, 'So it seems that our love is doomed, unless . . .'

'Doomed indeed,' Isabel said desolately. 'And I shall have to marry Sir Ralph.'

His arms tightened round her so fiercely that she gasped. 'I swear by my life I will not let him have you. Did you not hear me say "unless"? Unless you consent to come away with me to another country, where we could be married and live . . . Well, I do not know yet how we could live, but we would find a way.'

Isabel shook her head sadly.

'You know full well that we should be followed and brought back. There is but one way for me, and that is to refuse to be married against my will. But,' her voice trembled as doubts swept over her, 'my father is not yet strong enough to hear such bad news, and when he is recovered . . . Well, you know how stern he and my mother can be.'

'None the less'—Anthony said grimly—'if you truly love me, you must resist. When your father is well again, I shall speak with him. Together we shall . . .' He stopped suddenly, and turned as the side door opened and Alice stood in the moonlight, beckoning urgently.

Isabel pulled herself free, her heart beating wildly.

'She has heard something! Go quickly, Anthony. You must not be found here with me.'

'I shall come tomorrow with my father,' he said, and melted away into the shadows.

In the doorway Alice stood shivering with fear. 'I heard a sound. Someone is coming. What shall we do?'

It was too late to hide. A tall figure holding a candle was coming down the passage and, for a moment, Isabel thought it was her mother. Then, to her horror, she heard Sir Ralph Overton's voice.

'So, Mistress Isabel, you take a moonlight walk. I trust you are refreshed.'

She drew herself up haughtily. 'There was no need for you to spy on me, Sir Ralph. My maid and I sought the cool of the courtyard. Will you stand aside, if you please, and allow us to go back to our beds.'

'It seemed to me that you were alone in the courtyard, Mistress, while your maid kept guard for you. Or were you not alone?' Turning to Alice, he added, 'Go to your chamber, wench. I wish to talk with your mistress.'

With a gasp of terror, Alice fled, and Isabel made to follow, but Sir Ralph held her back.

Angrily she shook him off. 'How dare you give commands to my servant, sir? Let me pass at once.'

Suddenly she froze in alarm as the sound of a horse's whinny of welcome came from the garden. Recovering herself quickly, she turned to shut the door, then stood waiting for Sir Ralph to move aside. To her dismay he continued to block her way, then, placing the candle on a wide ledge, he reached out and gripped her shoulders fiercely.

'Mistress Isabel'—his voice was as hard as his steely hands—'tell me the name of the man you meet in secret while your maid keeps watch for you. I have the right to know.'

'You have no right, sir.' Aroused by his arrogance, she lost her fear and was conscious only of a burning anger. 'You and I have never been betrothed, and I will never marry you. Let me go at once. I wish to return to my bed.'

He released her and picked up the candle but, just as she took a step forward, his free hand shot out and pulled her cloak wide apart. Shocked into immobility, she stood naked in front of him, and slowly he lowered the candle, sweeping the light over her from head to foot. Then he let the cloak fall and, speechless with shame, she clasped it tightly round her.

'So . . .' His voice was icy cold. 'Your lover holds you tight in his arms, all yielding softness against his manhood. Who is this fortunate young man who has perhaps already stolen your maidenhood?'

She gasped in fury. 'How dare you, sir? I am no wanton! No man has ever . . .' Suddenly she went limp under his cruel grip and began to sob helplessly. 'Let me go, I beg you. You have shamed me enough.'

He relaxed his hold a little, and stood gazing into her eyes for what seemed an eternity, while the shadows cast by the candle stayed almost motionless on the wall behind him. Then he said, 'Get you gone then to your bed. We shall speak of this tomorrow. But first I shall put my seal on you so that you will never forget, in spite of your denial, that you and I are to be wed.'

His kiss was hard and long, and he held her so closely that she could feel his heart beating against her own. Then, once more, he pulled her cloak aside and his mouth moved slowly to her breasts. Terrified, she struggled wildly and, careless of the consequences, opened her mouth to scream for help. Before she could utter a sound, his hand pressed over her lips and he released her.

'Go quickly. The rest can wait till we are wed. But, remember . . .' His voice was grim as he turned to pick up the candle. 'Remember, my sweet and most desirable mistress, that you are promised to me and none other.'

There was little sleep for her that night. When, breathless from her stumbling flight upstairs, she entered her room at last, she found Alice wringing her hands and weeping with fear. Somehow Isabel managed to keep her feelings hidden and, after binding her maid to strict secrecy, she told her that she loved Anthony and had made it quite plain to Sir Ralph that she would never marry him. Then she dismissed Alice and climbed into bed. At first she lay rigid with misery and fear, but gradually a fierce anger swept over her, and with it came determination. Even if she could never be

Anthony's wife she would still resist all pressure put upon her to marry Sir Ralph. What would happen as a result of her defiance, she did not know. Disobedient daughters were sometimes beaten and confined to their rooms on a diet of bread and water—at least that was what she had heard—but she could not imagine her own parents, strict though they were, treating her in that way. Comforting herself with the thought that she would see Anthony in a few hours' time, she fell into an uneasy slumber.

In the morning only Alice commented on the dark shadows under her eyes. Her mother, preoccupied with the preparation of healing drinks for her husband, was too worried to notice her daughter's listless manner and, when Isabel went in to see her father, Lady Holstead said,

'There is nothing you can do here, Isabel, but you will help me by entertaining our guest. He will understand that I must be with your father.'

Reluctantly Isabel went down and found Sir Ralph in the great hall. Resisting a momentary impulse to flee his presence, she stood erect and unsmiling as he bowed gravely. Then, as he raised his head and held her gaze, she felt the blood rush to her face.

'I trust you slept well, Mistress?' His eyes glinted with mockery. 'Did you have sweet dreams of our wedding day or, better still, of our wedding night? I must confess my own thoughts dwell on it constantly. Even more so, now that I have seen what beauty awaits me.'

Involuntarily she turned away and, to her intense relief, saw her mother descending the staircase.

Lady Holstead smiled at Sir Ralph, then looked

at her daugher. 'Why, Isabel, you seem near to tears. But there is no need to be low-spirited. Your father will recover, never fear. 'Tis naught but exhaustion. Go now into the garden with Sir Ralph while it is yet cool.'

They walked at first between low boxed hedges bordering flower-beds, where the air was full of the scent of roses and honeysuckle; then, as they turned a corner into another part of the garden hidden from the house by tall yew hedges, she drew a long breath and stood still.

'Sir Ralph . . .' she began, but he put up his hand.

'Your pardon, Mistress, but I must speak first. I have to ask you forgiveness for my behaviour. It was unmannerly of me to distress and shame you. Will you be gracious and grant me absolution?'

His appeal was so unexpected that it unnerved her and he stood waiting in silence, gazing at her so seriously that she almost weakened in her resolve to hate him. Then, as she saw him hastily try to control a half-smile trembling on his lips, she spoke coldly.

'I would rather forget last night, but I must talk of it now, so that you may understand what is in my heart. I told you I would not marry you, and now I shall tell you why. I love someone else. Someone I have known since childhood. It was he who came last night to tell me that he had spoken to his father, and . . .' She paused. 'Well, that is another matter, but now I trust you will see that I cannot marry you.'

'Ah!' Sir Ralph nodded gravely. 'So that is the reason. You think you are bound to him in a childhood friendship.'

'It is not a childish thing . . .' She flushed. 'I tell you, sir, we love each other dearly and wish to marry.'

'Why, then . . .' Once more the dark eyes held that mocking glint that she had learnt to hate. 'Why does he come in secret to visit you? Does he perhaps know that you are promised to me?'

'No. It is because . . . Well, it is a foolish reason. His father is of the new religion and, being old, he cannot see that, for us, that is a small matter.'

'A small matter?' He frowned. 'I do not understand you, Mistress. It seems to me a very great matter indeed. If he had been a Catholic, and if, as you say, you love each other, I might have said, "Marry and be happy"—I would not wish to break two loving hearts. But now . . .' He shook his head gently. 'Mistress Isabel, you and I are of the same faith. Sweet Mistress, it is your duty to marry me.'

Isabel stared at him incredulously. 'You—you would have let me go if An—if he I love were a Catholic?'

He slowly considered her words. 'Yes, though unwillingly, for the more I know you, the more . . .' He paused. 'However, that is not the purpose. You must forget this young man.'

She looked at him aghast. Nothing, it seemed, would persuade him to abandon his plans, and with so much weighed against them how could she and Anthony ever hope for happiness?

Suddenly she shuddered as though a cold wind had swept over her, then said fiercely, 'You cannot force me, sir. You must look for a Catholic wife elsewhere.' And gathering up her skirts, she fled back to the house.

A few minutes later, from her window, she saw

him walking round to the stable yard. Was he perhaps going to give orders to the groom to make his horse ready for his departure? Fervently she hoped he had at last accepted her refusal. Knowing that she was safe, she could brave her parents' anger more easily.

She was determined to bring matters to a head when she went in to see her father, and found to her relief that he was much better.

Sitting up in bed, he greeted her jovially. 'Your mother tells me you have been walking in the garden with Sir Ralph. Tell me, daughter, do you find him to your liking?'

Isabel drew a long breath.

'I—I . . .' she hesitated, and then, to her dismay, Sir Nicholas nodded and swept on enthusiastically,

'He is a fine man, is he not? He does much work for our hunted priests, though this is for your ears only. Even in a household such as ours, one must still be careful.'

He broke off as Lady Holstead came into the room.

'My dear,' he looked at her in mock despair—'I cannot drink another posset. You have plied me with so many that my stomach rebels.'

His wife smiled and put down the pewter mug. 'It will do later,' she said calmly. 'It is a herbal brew of my own invention, and will be refreshing because it is cold.'

Sir Nicholas looked doubtful, then his face brightened as she went to stand beside him. 'You see, my love, I am quite recovered. Your sweet presence is all I need now.' He glanced over to where Isabel had seated herself on a low stool by the window. 'And you, my child, will be like your mother. Sir Ralph will steal half my treasure when he takes you from me.'

Isabel looked at him mutely, longing to carry out her resolution, yet unable to bring herself to break up these happy moments of reunion.

It might well, she told herself, cause a setback to her father's health; although he was gentle and loving now, she knew from past experience how quickly he could burst out in a rage.

At last she said, 'You will soon be well enough to receive visitors. Mr Norton and Anthony have said they will come this evening to welcome you home.'

'Good! Good!' he beamed at her. 'Mr Norton is a very pleasant neighbour. I look forward to his visit.' He turned to his wife, then suddenly he struck his forehead. 'Lord! I have forgotten to tell you—My dear, there will be another visitor this evening. Scold me if you must, but in my tired state it slipped my memory.'

Lady Holstead smiled. 'Who is this mysterious guest?'

'It is no mystery. On our way here yesterday we encountered a certain Mr Viner—a cousin of Sir Ralph's, and about his age. He told us he had business in this part of the country. He is contemplating buying some land and building a house. A very agreeable young man, and a Catholic too, though unfortunately, as Sir Ralph told me afterwards, he mixes his faith with politics. But that need not concern us. I invited him to stay here while Sir Ralph is with us, and I ask your pardon for not telling you sooner.'

His wife stroked his hand affectionately. 'Do not let it trouble you, my love. I shall go and see that a bedchamber is prepared.'

Isabel followed her mother out of the room, and as they went down the great staircase she caught sight of Sir Ralph, dressed in his riding-clothes, standing waiting for them.

Her heart began to beat fast. Was he about to tell her mother that, in view of her daughter's attitude towards him, he would now be leaving their house? Apprehensively, she watched him as he took off his hat and bowed.

'Lady Holstead, have I your permission to ask Mistress Isabel to accompany me? This countryside is new to me, and it would be most agreeable if she could be my guide.'

Lady Holstead nodded graciously, then gave a slight frown as she caught sight of Isabel's reluctant expression. 'I am sure it will be a pleasure for her,' she said calmly. 'But you will have to wait a little while, as she is not suitably dressed. Go and change, Isabel.' She dismissed her daughter firmly, and turned to her guest. 'Now, Sir Ralph, tell me of your cousin. My husband has just told me the good news of his coming to stay with us.'

When at last Isabel came down wearing her green riding-habit, her mother was alone.

'You have been slow,' she said sharply. 'Sir Ralph is waiting outside with Will and the horses. You must be more courteous towards him or he will think you are an ungracious country dolt.'

'I do not care what he thinks of me,' Isabel said impulsively. 'Oh, Mother! I do not want to marry him!'

There! It was said, and she braced herself to meet the anger to come but, to her surprise, Lady Holstead's expression softened.

'It is often thus, my dear. Maidenly fears

are natural, but you must not let them rule you. Hasten, now. We shall talk of this later.'

Isabel frowned unhappily as she went outside, then flushed suddenly as she met Sir Ralph's admiring gaze. Nodding her thanks to Will as he helped her to mount, she rode ahead in silence until Sir Ralph drew alongside.

'Will you show me the extent of your father's estate, Mistress? I have a reason for my request, which I will tell you later.'

She looked at him scornfully. 'It is plain to see that you have a reason, sir. You think that, if you marry me, one day this estate will be joined to yours and then you will be even richer than you are now.'

Throwing back his head, he laughed. 'You misjudge me, Mistress. The reason I wish to know this countryside is . . .' He paused. 'Well, as you must know, there are times when it is necessary for a priest to escape pursuit, and a certain Mr Grant—at least, that is the name by which he is known—will be saying Mass here shortly. Your lady mother told me that Sir Nicholas is very anxious for this, and all arrangements have been made. It will be necessary to take great precautions, especially now that your father has suffered imprisonment. He will be more than ever suspect.'

He stopped as Isabel turned to stare at him, her eyes wide with alarm. Frowning, he gazed back at her searchingly, then he continued, 'It seems to me, Mistress, that you have not been told much of the affairs of our country. It is very pleasant to live as you have done so far in this quiet rural state, but I do not think your parents should have kept you in ignorance of the perils all around. If you will bear with me, I shall tell you how things are with us Catholics. In January of this year a new Act was passed, as a result of which all who are caught harbouring priests in their houses are called traitors and are liable to a great fine and a year's imprisonment. The priest himself, if he is caught, is horribly tortured to make him divulge the names of his associates, and eventually dies a terrible death. What is more, a common informer is rewarded if he can betray a Catholic family to the Commissioners. So you see how careful we must all be—trusting no one who is not of the faith.'

Suddenly the bright morning seemed to turn cold and grey as, forgetful of her own problems, Isabel began to understand the dangers of the harsh world in which she lived. Almost despairingly, she said slowly, 'It seems to me that our cause is lost already. We can do nothing against such punitive opposition.'

'Fie, Mistress! You must not lose heart so easily. There is but one answer to persecution, and that is to fight it with all our might. We have our seminaries abroad, where many brave young men from this country are being trained to be priests. They are coming over here as missionaries willing to give their lives in the struggle for freedom. They need help, of course—horses and clothes—for they have to travel in disguise, and they must be warned of the spies around them when they travel from one Catholic household to another. They . . .'

'Ah!' Isabel caught her breath. 'That is what my father must have meant when he said that you did much for the hunted priests.'

'I?' Sir Ralph gave a light laugh, but his eyes narrowed angrily. 'Your father is mistaken if he thinks I seek martyrdom. He is also very indiscreet. I trust, Mistress, that you will not repeat his tale to others.'

She looked across at him scornfully. 'Have no fear, sir. You are quite plainly not so ardent for the faith that you would put your life in danger.'

For a moment he gazed at her, and then he smiled.

'You have a poor opinion of me, Mistress! But perhaps, when we are married, you will come to tolerate my human weaknesses.' He reined in his horse. 'Tell me—Down there in the valley, is that a Catholic house?'

Isabel's face flamed in alarm as she realised that, all unconsciously, she had led the way to Vale Court. For a moment she hesitated, all too aware that Sir Ralph had seen her agitation. As calmly as she could, she said, 'That is where Mr Norton lives. He and his son are good friends to us, although they are Protestants.'

He looked at her gravely, 'Your father spoke of them to me on our journey here. The son—he is called Anthony, I believe.' He paused, his eyes on her hot cheeks. 'I see from the colour in your face, Mistress, that I have discovered your secret. This Master Anthony is the man you love, is he not?'

Turning in the saddle, she stared at him coldly but said nothing.

For a few minutes they continued to ride in silence until, at last, he said quietly, 'It is cool under these trees. Let me help you down. We shall sit for a while and talk at our ease.'

While he tethered the horses she stood gazing sorrowfully at Vale Court. So much had happened since she had sat peacefully in the Mews with Anthony. Now her whole world was in turmoil, and the future seemed desolate and forbidding.

'Do not look so troubled, Mistress.' Sir Ralph stood beside her. 'Come, sit here . . .' He spread his cloak on a grassy hillock, and unwillingly she sank down, turning her head away as he sat beside her. At last he said slowly, his voice full of compassion, 'I am indeed sorry that you cannot marry him. But you must see that it is only a dream—A dream that you must forget.'

'Why?' She turned to him wildly. 'Why do you persist in this fashion? You talk of freedom— Anthony is a Protestant, but he would never take me away from my faith. It is our parents who hold these old ideas. They . . .'

'Mistress? Have you not listened to what I have been saying?' Sir Ralph shook his head in despair. 'Your parents are aware of the dangers to come. That is why they are glad that you will be under my protection. I am in favour with the Queen—my father was able to be of service to her when she was in the Tower and suffering from her sister Mary's displeasure. Although it is known that I am a Catholic, the Queen still allows me to attend Court so long as I do not parade my religion. Together, you and I shall found a new Catholic family and play our part in keeping the faith alive in England.'

Isabel felt the blood drain from her face. It seemed that Sir Ralph was intent only on fulfilling his duty, and that, for him, marriage was but a means to an end. She realised suddenly that he was watching her intently, waiting for her to speak and, at last, in a low voice, she said, 'A marriage without love—That is not my idea of happiness.'

'Love!' He smiled wryly. 'Can you think no further than that? Even suppose I were not here, your parents would still forbid you to marry this Protestant. So what would you do in your pursuit of happiness? Fly with him to a strange land? Abandon your family and your country, leaving all behind you that you hold dear? Is your love as great as that?'

She jumped up suddenly and stood with her eyes fixed on Vale Court, as though willing Anthony to come to her assistance. Then she turned and looked down at the man gazing at her, his mouth twisted in a cynical smile.

'Yes,' she said steadily, 'my love is strong enough for that.'

He gave a short exclamation and rose in his turn, towering over her angrily. For a moment she thought he was about to take her in his arms again and, dismayed and frightened, took a step back. But he made no move to touch her. Instead, he said furiously,

'I am no saint, Mistress. I can stand no more of this childish talk. You think you love deeply, but it is merely a maiden's fancy for a callow youth. I shall teach you the meaning of a good marriage. You will soon forget your Anthony when you hold our babe to your breast. Now let us finish our ride.'

Her face flaming with humiliation, she was obliged to allow him to help her mount but, once in the saddle, she turned the mare and urged her into a gallop, recklessly heading for Vale Court. Desperately she raced on, heedless of the consequences, knowing only that she must see Anthony and ask for his help. Turning to look behind, she saw that Sir Ralph was chasing after her but, measuring the distance, she knew there was a good chance that she would get there first. She would leave the mare at the great gates and then, hidden by the wall, she could slip round to the Mews, hoping that Anthony would be there.

But the ground was uneven, and just as she reached the gates the mare stumbled and, with a cry, Isabel fell heavily to the ground. Frantically she tried to get up but, tangled in her riding-clothes, she had only just got to her feet when Sir Ralph pulled up beside her.

Looking up at him she saw such anger in his eyes that she began to shiver violently but, unexpectedly, his voice was gentle.

'Sit here and rest a while. It is the shock that makes you tremble.'

Settling her with her back against the wall, he took off his cloak and wrapped it round her. For a minute she sat in silence, then she said impatiently,

'I am not hurt. It is not the first time I have taken a tumble.' Handing him back his cloak, she rose and looked at him steadily. 'I had thought to escape, sir, but I see there is nothing for it but to ride back home. If you wish to explore further, you must go alone or get Will to accompany you.'

He nodded, his face set hard as he brought up her mare; then, just as they were about to move off, there was a sound of voices, and the gates opened. A manservant stood waiting, and a moment later Anthony rode out.

He stared, his face alight with joy at the sight of Isabel, then he frowned as he saw her companion.

Sir Ralph swept off his plumed riding hat and said pleasantly, 'Master Anthony Norton, I think. I am Ralph Overton—a guest of Sir Nicholas Holstead.'

'How do you do, sir?' Anthony's eyes were on Isabel's troubled face. 'You were, I hope, coming to call on us?'

Before Sir Ralph could answer, Isabel said urgently, 'Anthony, I must speak with you!' She glanced at Sir Ralph coldly—'Alone.'

Sir Ralph shrugged and wheeled his horse away, and Isabel waited until he was out of earshot, while Anthony gazed at her in astonishment.

'What is this?' he asked anxiously. 'Why are you so distressed? Will you not come into the house with me?'

'No. There is no time. Oh, Anthony! Sir Ralph is determined to marry me, and I fear greatly that he will have his way if we do not act quickly. You asked me to go away with you across the sea—I am sure now that it is our only hope.' She hesitated. 'I am so fearful and troubled in my mind that I do not know what else can be done, but perhaps . . .' She looked at him searchingly. 'Perhaps it is asking too much of you, for you will lose everything and gain only me.'

He laughed joyously and her heart lifted in gratitude as her moment of doubt passed.

'It is the only way, my sweet. Without you, I have nothing. I shall make plans, and this evening, when we come to visit your father, I shall tell you what you must do. Put your trust in me, and do not be afraid.'

She nodded thankfully, and turned as Sir Ralph approached. Raising his hat once more, he smiled grimly, and Anthony calmly acknowledged the salute.

'We shall meet this evening, sir,' he said coldly. 'Goodbye, Mistress Isabel.'

CHAPTER
THREE

CLOUDS WERE gathering as Isabel and Sir Ralph
arrived in sight of Holstead Hall. It had been a
silent ride, with Sir Ralph deep in thought. Isabel's
mind was filled half with joy at Anthony's strength
and resolution and half with a frightening vision of
all that flight across the sea would entail.

The lowering skies seemed to reflect her fears
and, as they dismounted in the stable yard, she
could hear rumbles of thunder in the distance.

Sir Ralph glanced up. 'My cousin is likely to get
soaked, which will not please him overmuch,' he
remarked lightly as they walked towards the house.

Isabel frowned. She had forgotten all about the
arrival of their unknown guest. Still, she reflected,
it would perhaps be a fortunate distraction.
Another visitor to engage her parents in conversation might enable her to steal a few moments
alone with Anthony in the evening.

Sir Ralph glanced at her quizzically. 'You do not
look pleased, Mistress, and I myself am not overwhelmed with joy at the prospect of Henry's company during my stay in your house.'

In spite of her resolve to avoid conversation with
him, she could not contain her curiosity. 'Why,
then, if you are not good friends, did you allow my
father to invite him?'

'I could not gainsay him.' He smiled wryly. 'Your father, in his generosity, thought he was giving me pleasure.' For a moment, he was silent. 'It is not that Henry and I are enemies; merely that we do not look at events in the same way. He thinks I am too loyal to the Queen, whereas he maintains that she is a usurper with no legitimate right to the throne. He is for the Queen of Scots, who, according to him, should also be Queen of England.'

'But Queen Elizabeth was King Henry's daughter.' Isabel looked bewildered. 'I do not see that the Queen of Scots has any right to the throne.'

'My cousin contends—and there are many who agree with him—that Elizabeth, having been born to Anne Bullen while Henry's rightful wife Catherine was alive, is but a bastard with no legal right to the throne. The Queen of Scots, as Henry's great-niece, should have succeeded.'

Isabel nodded thoughtfully, her interest unwillingly aroused by this man who talked to her of great events in the world outside—events that her parents never spoke of in her presence. Pondering aloud, she said,

'But now that Queen Elizabeth has been crowned and acknowledged for so long as our rightful sovereign, surely we owe her our allegiance? It is true that she persecutes her Catholic subjects, but that should not stop us from being loyal to her as our anointed queen.'

Sir Ralph stopped and stared at her. 'You are a quick pupil, Mistress. You have looked clearly at the problem, and solved it in a fashion that is entirely to my own way of thinking.'

She flushed. Praise such as this was a new experience, and for a moment she glowed with pleasure.

Then, quickly, she turned away. It was one thing to talk of loyalty to the Queen, but what of her loyalty to Anthony? She must not, she told herself, allow this man's flattery to win her over.

As they entered the house, Lady Holstead greeted them with a smiling face.

'Sir Nicholas has left his bed and declares that he will eat with us in the summer parlour,' she announced. 'He says he is fully recovered, though I myself would have preferred him to rest a little longer. We shall dine a little later than usual, however, as one of the servants, on an errand for me, has just returned with the news that Mr Viner is but a few miles away.' She turned to Isabel. 'Go quickly, my love, and change your dress so as to be ready to receive our visitor.'

Alice was waiting in the bedchamber, and when Isabel had washed her face and hands, she said, 'Oh, Mistress! I am dying of curiosity. Does Sir Ralph accept meekly your refusal to marry him? From what I hear, he does not seem downcast.'

'"From what I hear"!' Isabel turned furiously. 'Alice, have you dared to talk of this matter with the other servants?'

'No, Mistress. I swear I only listened to their gossiping. I would never betray you . . .' She looked at Isabel reproachfully. 'I long for you to be happy.'

Isabel looked searchingly into Alice's clear blue eyes, which were slowly filling with tears, then impulsively she clasped the girl in her arms. 'Do not distress yourself, Alice. That you are a true friend, I do not doubt.' Her voice trembled. 'I may indeed need your help, but you must wait until I can tell you more. Anthony is coming here tonight, and I do not know yet what he has planned.'

'Mistress . . .' Alice hesitated, then said slowly, 'I am puzzled. I understand that you feel resentful towards Sir Ralph, but are you not perhaps a little blind? If you had not loved Master Anthony, would you not have found Sir Ralph all that is desirable in a husband? He is handsome, he has much charm and wit—his servants constantly extol his virtues— and he is a good Catholic, whereas . . .' She stopped at the sight of her mistress's quick frown.

With an effort, Isabel held back her irritation. Alice meant well, and it was natural that she should be impressed by Sir Ralph's self-confidence and air of prosperity.

'You do not understand,' she said at last. Then, seeing that Alice was about to argue, she added briskly, 'Now we must not waste time in talking. I shall wear my white silk dress—it will be cooler in this heat.'

Obediently Alice set about her task, and at last Isabel was ready and stood surveying herself in the silver-framed mirror. The maid said, 'You are beautiful indeed, Mistress. I am not surprised that two men should both love you.'

'Two?' Isabel turned in surprise. 'Sir Ralph does not love me. He is but fulfilling what he deems to be his duty. A Catholic wife—a Catholic family—all planned by his parents and mine.'

'It could bring happiness,' Alice said gently. 'I also think that, in spite of what you say, Sir Ralph is very near to loving you. I know the signs.'

'You know . . . ?' Isabel looked at her doubt-fully. 'What do you know of love, Alice?'

The maid flushed. 'I shall tell you, Mistress,' she

said at last. 'I love Will Rayner, and he loves me.'
She paused. 'I have not told you before, but since
we are talking of such things I would not like you to
think I do not understand your feelings. One day I
hope to be Will's wife. I love him with all my heart.'

Surprised and touched at the girl's calm dignity,
Isabel put her arm round Alice's shoulder. 'Dear
Alice—I wish you all happiness. I never guessed;
but, now that I know, it makes another bond
between us.'

Suddenly there was a sound of voices outside,
and Isabel went to the window.

'Sir Ralph's cousin has arrived,' she said quickly.
'I must go.'

Mr Viner, dusty and travel-stained, was greeted
kindly by Lady Holstead and Sir Nicholas, while
Isabel studied him with interest. A year or two
younger than his cousin, he was undeniably handsome with a strong resemblance to Sir Ralph, but
his eyes were set rather closely together and
seemed cold and wary in spite of the fact that
he smiled charmingly while making courteous
conversation.

Suddenly, as they were talking, a flash of light-
ning lit up the hall followed almost immediately by
a tremendous crash of thunder. Startled, Isabel
jumped and turned quickly, almost colliding with
Sir Ralph. To her annoyance he put his arm protectively round her shoulder but, recovering instantly,
she frowned and pulled herself free. Then, as he
strolled over to the window to watch the progress of
the storm, she became aware of a thoughtful gaze
fixed on her from the other side of the room. Mr
Viner's keen eyes, it seemed, were quick to notice
small things. Meeting her glance, he gave a half-

smile and, to her surprise, she realised that he had enjoyed seeing his cousin rebuffed.

The storm grew in intensity and the oak furniture was hardly visible against the panelled walls. Only the vivid colours of rich clothes relieved the gloom, while the rain poured from the guttering and dashed against the window-panes.

Later, when they had finished eating and were sitting in the comfort of Lady Holstead's chamber, Sir Nicholas uttered aloud the fear that was growing in Isabel's mind.

'I do not think Mr Norton and his son will be able to visit us this evening,' he said. 'It seems that this storm will continue through the day.'

Lady Holstead agreed, and turned to her guests. 'Our good neighbours from Vale Court,' she said in explanation. 'Unfortunately they are of the new religion, but we have never let that come between us.'

'Or ever shall,' said Sir Nicholas heartily. 'Mr Norton was most sympathetic to my wife when I was in the Tower. He sent his servant over with offers of help, and expressed his great regret that I should have to suffer for my beliefs.'

'A very rare friendship,' commented Mr Viner drily. 'Let us hope it will not be strained too far. I have seen too many Catholic plans betrayed by good Protestant friends to put my trust in heretics.'

Isabel's face flushed in anger, but a quick glance from her mother stopped her from indignantly refuting this disapproving criticism.

Sir Nicholas frowned. 'Maybe, maybe. Nevertheless, I do trust Mr Norton. However,' he added thoughtfully, 'I do not confide in him when we have the happiness of a visit from a priest. We are careful in this household, and our servants are all good Catholics.'

'As good as they can be,' Lady Holstead sighed. 'They too are liable to be fined if they do not attend the parish church, and we have to increase their wages so that they can pay this most unjust imposition.'

'It is not right that we should remain inactive under such persecution,' said Mr Viner bitterly. 'If all the Catholics in the country could be made to rise and fight, we could oust this pretended queen from her throne and install our rightful sovereign— Mary, Queen of Scotland and England.'

For a long moment there was silence, and Sir Nicholas, shocked at such wild talk, glanced uneasily at his wife. Then Sir Ralph said icily,

'Cousin, you do naught but harm to our cause by such treasonable ranting. To talk of overthrowing our anointed Queen—for that you could be put to death, a death you would undoubtedly deserve. Such disloyalty shames our family, who have always served the Crown faithfully.'

Mr Viner flushed, but before he could make any riposte, Lady Holstead looked up from her embroidery.

'Isabel—I think a little music would be agreeable to us all.'

She looked meaningly at a lute standing in a corner of the room, and, unable to refuse, Isabel picked it up reluctantly. But as the first rippling notes sounded through the room, there was a sudden commotion from below and, a moment later a servant knocked and came in.

'Your pardon, my lady,' he said nervously. 'But there is a fellow below who says he comes from

Kent with a message for Sir Ralph.' He paused. 'Shall I bring him up here?'

Sir Ralph rose quickly to his feet. 'No, I shall go down and speak with him. Will you excuse me, ladies?'

As he left the room, Mr Viner frowned and turned to Sir Nicholas.

'I fear some mishap may have occurred. The village near my cousin's estate is very zealous in the new religion, and I have heard rumours that Catholic houses have been attacked while their owners are away. I would not like to see his house in ruins—I spent many happy hours there with him when we were children.'

Sir Nicholas sighed heavily. 'What times we live in! Will they ever get better, I wonder?'

'I do not think so . . .' Mr Viner answered slowly. 'That is why I am for the Catholic Queen of Scots. It is either that, or we shall all have to become Protestants if we do not want to lose everything we possess. I tell you, sir, we must rebel against this monstrous Act which turns us into traitors. There are plans afoot . . .' He stopped suddenly as the door opened. 'Ah, Ralph—What is the news?'

Sir Ralph frowned. 'It is not good. The villagers set fire to my house. Happily, my steward and the servants repelled them and put out the fire before much damage was done, and there the matter rests.' He turned to Lady Holstead. 'I fear, however, that I must go away for a few days. Have I your leave to return here when I have put my affairs in order?'

She smiled. 'But of course. We shall look forward to your return.'

'Shall I come with you, cousin?' Mr Viner looked searchingly at Sir Ralph. 'My business here can wait, and possibly I could be of some assistance.'

'Thank you, Henry, but it is not necessary for me to take you away from this pleasant company. I shall deal speedily with this small matter.'

The storm was at last dying out when Sir Ralph said goodbye, and Isabel, who had remained upstairs alone, was gazing out of the window when she heard Mr Viner enter the room.

'Your lady mother is with your father in the oak parlour and asks you to join them,' he said. Then, looking at her meaningfully, he added, 'They are planning the date of your marriage. I overheard them talking with my cousin in the hall.' He sighed affectedly. 'Ah, how fortunate is Ralph to be betrothed to one so beautiful!'

Isabel's eyes widened in anger. 'Mr Viner—I think you should know that I am not willing to marry your cousin. I have already told him, but he seems unable to understand. I can see that I must make the matter clear to my parents.'

'You surprise me, Mistress.' Mr Viner's eyebrows rose in astonishment. 'Do you not find Ralph a congenial companion? And do you not realise how rich and influential he is? I should have thought . . .' He studied her thoughtfully. 'Well, it is good news to me, and I wish you success in your resistance.'

Isabel stared at him in surprise. 'Why does my decision please you, sir?'

He shrugged, and stroked his beard with a strange, almost calculating look in his eyes. Then he said slowly, 'To be frank, Mistress Isabel, I have long entertained a rather forlorn hope that my esteemed cousin would either remain celibate or perhaps even become a priest.' He smiled faintly as he saw her bewilderment. 'You do not understand? Well, I shall enlighten you. If my cousin dies without legitimate issue then I, as his heir, shall inherit his estates.' He looked at her quizzically. 'And as I have many debts, and am likely to accumulate more . . .' He laughed lightly at the shocked expression on Isabel's face. 'Ah, Mistress—you must not scorn me for coveting my cousin's possessions. He knows full well that I envy him, but I also love him like a brother and would never wish him harm.'

She stared at him in wonder. What a strange man he was!

'I think your hopes are in vain, sir. Your cousin is very desirous of a wife, and even though I reject him he will no doubt soon find success elsewhere. But why did you mention the priesthood? I should not have thought him a likely candidate for martyrdom.'

He laughed. 'Perhaps not, Mistress. But he travels much to France on mysterious business. I had begun to think that he might be considering giving up the world and becoming a Jesuit, but then, when I heard of his betrothal . . .'

'There is no betrothal, or ever has been,' Isabel said sharply. 'But . . .' She smiled derisively. 'Sir Ralph a priest? That is beyond belief.'

'Then why does he go so often to France? He has, I know, some family connection on his mother's side—she was herself French—but I do not think . . .' He shook his head slowly and added, almost to himself, 'I would dearly love to discover his business.'

'Perhaps . . .' Isabel began, then stopped

abruptly. It was no affair of hers what Sir Ralph did in France, and she had no interest in discussing his movements with his cousin.

'Perhaps?' Mr Viner prompted her gently, but she shrugged carelessly.

'Perhaps he has a mistress over there,' she said lightly.

He smiled a little scornfully, and dismissed the idea with a shake of his head.

She turned away. 'I must leave you, sir, and go to my parents.'

A few minutes later, when she entered the oak parlour, she was greeted sharply by her mother.

'Sit down, Isabel. Why have you been so slow? We have important matters to discuss with you.'

Pulling up a joined stool, Isabel sat down and folded her hands in her lap, seemingly calm but inwardly dreading the ordeal she must now face.

Seated erect in their oak panel back armchairs, her parents looked awesome, like judges about to pronounce sentence on their prisoner. They were very dear to her, but there was fear mingled with her affection. She had always been treated kindly—even, at times, indulgently—but respect for their authority had been implanted in her since babyhood.

Lady Holstead frowned slightly as she smoothed out a crease in her black and ivory silk gown, then turned to her husband, who cleared his throat.

'Sir Ralph has suggested that, on his return from Kent, we should take advantage of Mr—er—Grant's visit and ask him to perform the marriage ceremony.' He stopped as he saw Isabel's face go deathly pale. 'Yes—I know. It is a pity that it must all be done so quickly. Your mother would have liked more time in which to make the proper preparations for assembling your wedding clothes, but Sir Ralph feels that we must take this opportunity. Lord knows when we shall have another.' He held up his hand as Isabel opened her mouth to speak. 'No, daughter. It cannot be delayed. Sir Ralph is right, and you must not make difficulties. The marriage must be in secret, for the law lays down that all weddings must be performed by a minister of the new religion and take place in the parish church. This is a law we are forced to disobey.'

Isabel drew a long shuddering breath. 'Father, I must tell you now. I cannot marry Sir Ralph. I love another man.'

For a few moments there was a terrible silence. Sir Nicholas stared speechlessly at his daughter, while a slow flush of anger mounted to his forehead, and Lady Holstead put her hand to her cheek as though she had been struck.

'What? What?' At last Sir Nicholas found his voice. 'You cannot—another man—what nonsense is this? Wife'—he turned abruptly—'do you understand the wench?'

Lady Holstead shook her head, her eyes fixed in horrified amazement on her daughter. 'I know naught of this. Are you mad, Isabel? Who is this man you say you love?'

Isabel's heart was beating so furiously that it seemed to rise in her throat and choke her but, at last, she forced herself to speak.

'Anthony Norton.' At the sound of his name, courage suddenly swept over her. Head erect, she looked her father steadily in the face. 'He and I love each other dearly, and he has asked me to marry him.'

'Anthony . . . ? By God!' Sir Nicholas gripped the arms of his chair. 'Now I know your mother is right. You have lost your wits!'

Suddenly he gave a harsh laugh and turned to his wife.

'Do not look so nervous, my dear. It is of no account. It is but a maiden's folly . . .' His eye-brows drew together in a terrible frown. 'And a young man's scheming. I had thought better of Anthony, but it seems that he has taken advantage of my absence to sow mischief.' He pointed to the door. 'To your room, Mistress, and count yourself fortunate that I do not beat you into submission. But submit you will, and swiftly. Nay'—he inter-cepted Isabel's quick glance at her mother, who sat rigid and white-faced in her chair—'you will have no mercy there. Get you gone! I will not speak with you until you beg my forgiveness.'

An hour later, dry-eyed and stiff with shock, Isabel was on her bed when the door opened softly and her mother came cautiously into the room.

'My poor daughter'—Lady Holstead stroked the girl's wet cheek—'try not to be so sad. At least you are not to be confined to your room on a diet of bread and water, as I was when I was only sixteen and tried to resist my parents' will.' She smiled ruefully, and Isabel gazed at her incredulously.

'You, Mother? You were a rebel, too?'

Lady Holstead nodded reminiscently. 'Yes. But I was beaten and made to suffer grievously until I consented to marry your father. I was homesick, too, for many a day; but it passed, and my dislike turned to love—as it so often does, and as I am sure it will do in your case.'

Isabel turned her head away despondently. 'Oh,

Mother! I thought you were going to offer me help, but you seem as fixed as my father in your determination to marry me to Sir Ralph.'

Lady Holstead looked calmly at her. 'I have tried to comfort you with the benefit of my own experience. I believe that Sir Ralph is the right man for you. Anthony . . .' She paused as the colour rose in Isabel's face. 'Anthony is a good lad, but you could never be happy as his wife. The division between you would widen with the years. Your children would be a cause of much dispute.' She shrugged her shoulders sadly. 'You must see, Isabel, that your father and I could never give consent to such a match.'

Slowly Isabel fell back among the pillows. 'So I am to stay here until I marry Sir Ralph?' she asked desolately.

Her mother smiled and shook her head. 'Not so. I have prevailed on your father to let you join us as usual. But you must be very courteous to him, for he is extremely angry.'

Isabel shook her head. 'I would rather stay here. Thank you for interceding for me, Mother, but I do not want it to seem as though I am about to submit.'

'But you must, daughter!' Lady Holstead pulled herself erect, her manner suddenly stern and forbidding. 'I have done my best, but now I see you have no love for us or you would not act so wickedly. I will leave you to think over my words.' At the door she turned, and added coldly, 'Wash your face and see to your hair. If you do not wish to enrage your father even more, you will join us as speedily as possible.'

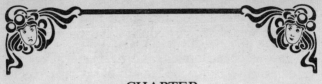

CHAPTER
FOUR

To ANTHONY, riding through the steady rain that evening, the sudden change in the weather was a godsend. He had been gazing moodily out of the window when his father said,

'It is not an evening for visiting, I fear. Sir Nicholas will not expect us.' Then, as Anthony turned impatiently, Mr Norton added gently, 'If you wish to go alone, you have my permission.' His voice grew stern. 'But this talk of marriage between you and Mistress Isabel is not to be mentioned. Do you understand?'

'Only too well, sir,' Anthony said bitterly. 'You have convinced me that you and Isabel's parents, divided as you are in religion, will be united in preventing our future happiness.'

'Dear lad,' Mr Norton gazed at his son pityingly, 'you and I have been good friends up till now and I regret with all my heart that I have to stand against you in this matter.' He paused. 'I have been pondering the subject, and I think you should go away for a while. I shall write to your uncle William and ask him to take you into his household for a few months. He would, I am sure, welcome your help in running his estate, and your cousins would be pleased to have your company.'

Anthony shrugged indifferently. It was obvious

that his father hoped he would find consolation among the several girl cousins and their friends, and that their charms would take his mind off Isabel. How little he understood, after all! But the prospect of being sent away made it all the more imperative to formulate a plan for escape. He had spoken confidently enough that morning to Isabel but, in reality, his mind was in a turmoil. The enormity of what he had suggested was becoming plain. The way ahead was fraught with difficulties. How could they survive in a foreign land? He had no skills other than those of a country gentleman, and no friends to whom he could turn for help. Desperately, he considered the dilemma, but was no nearer a solution when he arrived at last at Holstead Hall.

Will, called down from his quarters over the stables, watched in silence as Anthony dismounted, then, as he took over the horse, said, 'It is good to see you, Master Anthony.' He hesitated for a moment, then added confidentially, 'You will not, I fear, have the pleasure of meeting Sir Ralph Overton this evening. He has had to go back to his house in Kent on urgent business.'

Anthony stared, then, murmuring something non-committal, he made his way round to the house. Suddenly his spirits rose. Sir Ralph must have admitted defeat and taken his leave in high dudgeon. Perhaps Isabel's parents would be more favourably inclined to his suit now that the rich suitor was off the scene.

There was no sign of anything untoward when the servant admitted him into the house, and when he entered the withdrawing chamber, all seemed calm.

Lady Holstead was reading her herbal, Sir Nicholas was sitting deep in thought and Isabel was occupied with her embroidery. A gentleman was seated near her and, for a moment, Anthony looked aghast, thinking that Will had been mistaken and that Sir Ralph had not gone away. But as he moved further into the room he saw that this man was a stranger.

Then, as he bowed to the company, he realised with a sickening shock that, in spite of the apparently peaceful scene, there was after all something very wrong. Instead of the kindly welcome Anthony usually received, Sir Nicholas and his wife gazed at him coldly and Isabel stared at him in unmistakable alarm.

Sir Nicholas turned stiffly towards his daughter. 'Isabel, take Mr Viner into the long gallery, if you please. I wish to talk to Master Anthony.'

The stranger rose and bowed, and Isabel glanced piteously at Anthony as the door closed behind them. Sir Nicholas said harshly,

'What is your business here, sir?'

'Why—Why . . .' The blood drained from Anthony's face. 'I came to congratulate you, Sir Nicholas, on your return home and make my excuses for my father who, not being strong, could not venture out in this rain.' He stopped, his bewilderment increasing as Sir Nicholas glared at him.

'I would rather have spoken with your father but, since he is not here, I will be plain with you. You may no longer regard yourself as our friend, sir. You have taken advantage of my absence to fill my daughter's head with rebellion against her parents.' His voice rose angrily. 'You have dared to talk to her of marriage—a marriage that you know full well could never be allowed. You are a knave, Master Anthony, or, at best, a fool.'

His fingers drummed angrily on the arms of his chair, and Lady Holstead glanced at him anxiously. She turned to Anthony, 'You have caused us much sorrow,' she said reproachfully, but there was compassion in her eyes as she looked at the young man, his face drawn and pale, standing shocked into speechlessness.

At last, with a great effort, he found his voice.

'My lady—Sir Nicholas. Mistress Isabel and I love each other dearly. If we could marry I would never stand in the way of her religion. We—Oh, sir!' His voice broke. 'I swear I would make her happy and, if you would relent, then my father might . . .' He stopped abruptly as Sir Nicholas held up his hand.

'Love? What has that to do with such a grave matter as marriage?' he asked scornfully. Then, seeing Anthony's hands clench together, he added a shade more gently, 'I am sorry indeed that things have come to this pass but you must put all thoughts of marriage out of your mind. Hitherto you have always been welcome in our house, but I must ask you to stay away in future. Isabel will marry Sir Ralph, and she must not be encouraged in her rebellious attitude. When she has left this house as his wife, you will be welcome here once more.'

Anthony bowed stiffly and turned to leave. Then he paused at the door. 'May I have your permission, sir, to say goodbye to Mistress Isabel?'

Sir Nicholas shook his head sternly. 'No. Our daughter has been told that there will be no further meetings.'

Dismissed so ruthlessly, Anthony hesitated outside the door. Isabel had gone through the side door into the long gallery, and there was no way in which he could get to her. Disconsolately, he began to descend the stairs when, to his surprise, he saw Alice in the hall below, standing still as though waiting for him.

She curtsied quickly. 'Mistress Isabel told me to give you this, sir.' She looked cautiously around, then handed him a letter. 'If you wish to answer it, Will Rayner, who is my friend, will pass on your message to me.'

Anthony nodded and thrust the letter into his doublet, but before he could thank her, Alice had curtsied again and sped up the staircase.

Will was waiting with Anthony's horse as though he had guessed that the visit would be short, and as the young man leapt into the saddle the groom asked quietly, 'Have you seen Alice, sir?'

'Yes. She has told me that you are to be trusted to take messages. I thank you heartily, for Mistress Isabel and I shall need friends.'

Will grinned sympathetically, and as Anthony gathered up the reins he said, 'May I speak my mind, sir?'

Anthony nodded, and Will said quietly,

'Alice and I love Mistress Isabel. We desire her happiness above all, but we do not think it would be wise if you and she did anything foolhardy, such as . . .' He hesitated, his eyes troubled, and then burst out, 'Do not take her away, Master Anthony. It would be madness—her good name lost—her whole future uncertain . . .' He stopped as he saw the expression on Anthony's face. 'Well, sir, I have said I will pass messages, but I shall not help in any scheme that would, in the end, ruin my mistress.'

Anthony sat silent, staring down at the man's worried face. After a moment, he shook up the reins and moved away.

Once out in the open, he drove his heels into the horse's side and began to ride like a madman. At last he slowed down and felt inside his doublet. Perhaps Isabel had a better plan than the wild idea he had at first suggested. Will was right: to run away with her was madness. Isabel would be the one to bear the worst suffering. Life in some squalid lodging, children born to live in poverty—he had no right to drag his dear love down to that level.

With a heavy heart he rode back home and, in the safety of his own room, opened the letter. Sitting on the side of his bed, he read it through twice and buried his face in his hands. She was willing to do anything he suggested—she would go with him to the ends of the earth—but she had no plan, no real understanding of what such a flight would mean.

He got up and paced about the room trying vainly to visualise the future. Then he stopped and picked up the letter again. What had she said at the end—Ah! here it was.

'One thing I will never do, and that is to marry Sir Ralph. My parents may punish me—I do not care. No marriage would be valid if I refused to consent, so I shall hold out for ever, if need be.'

Anthony stared down at the hastily-written phrase. This, then, was the solution. This was their only hope. If Isabel could resist long enough, her parents and his father might eventually give in. Better still, the religious enmity now prevailing in the country might relax.

He resumed his pacing, thinking of the way things were moving in public affairs. If, as the rumour had it, the Queen should marry her latest suitor, a Frenchman—the Duke d'Alençon—her 'Little Frog' as she called him, on account of his stature and unattractive appearance, with the example of a Protestant married to a Catholic, things were bound to become easier. It was said that the Duke was coming back to England in the autumn, and that the Queen would then announce her decision. Never before had she been so serious in a courtship, and although the Duke was many years younger than she was, she did not apparently consider that a disadvantage. Soon it would be too late for her to produce an heir to the throne, so it was more than probable that she would take this tenacious young Frenchman as her husband. And yet—Anthony frowned to himself—it seemed unbelievable. After all these years of resisting pressure from her advisers, why should Elizabeth at last consent to marry? She must be forty-seven at least—a dangerous if not impossible age for her to bear a child. So, was it all once more a diplomatic courtship doomed to come to nothing? In that case, Anthony thought despondently, there would be no reason for religious tolerance and Catholics and Protestants would remain at loggerheads.

Next morning, after a restless night, he set off for Holstead Hall. The sun was shining once more and the countryside, refreshed after the heavy rain, looked so beautiful that Anthony's natural optimism returned. Life surely could not be as black and hopeless as it had seemed last night. The letter he was going to deliver to Will would make his views clear to Isabel. Perhaps, if luck were with him, he might even catch a glimpse of her, though he would have to be careful to avoid being seen by any member of the household. If only he himself had a servant whom he could trust to carry messages to Will; but his father's men were all Protestants, and there was no close friendship between them and the servants at Holstead Hall.

He pulled on the reins, slowing his horse down to a walk as a thought struck him. About two months ago there had been some talk of trouble with his Master Falconer, Dick Benton. The fellow had been having clandestine meetings with Lady Holstead's tirewoman. The other servants had informed Anthony's father, who had spoken gravely to Dick, and the affair must have come to nothing. Master Falconer was a strange, secretive man. An expert in dealing with hawks, subduing their ferocity and training them to perfection, he was not given to confidences, even with Anthony who shared the same interest. It was odd that a man who held strong Puritan views—views that even the Rector thought were extreme—should ever have contemplated a match with a papist; but love, as he knew only too well, was more powerful than religious differences. Perhaps, in spite of Dick's apparent obedience to his master, he was still seeing the girl and, if that were the case, he might be willing to help by passing on information and messages.

Leaving his horse in the field that marked the boundary of the two properties, Anthony made his way through the woods and was just emerging from the shade of the trees when he stopped. A man on horseback was coming out of the side gate. His heart leapt as he recognised Will. He waved quickly, then, slipping back into the cover of the woods, stood waiting.

A few minutes later Will appeared, leading his horse, and looked round cautiously as he approached. 'I am glad to see you, sir,' he said, holding out a letter. 'I was on my way to Vale Court, but I can ill spare the time. I think we must plan better than this if there are to be many such errands.'

Anthony nodded impatiently. 'I shall see what I can do, but first I must read what Mistress Isabel has to say.'

Will turned away and led his horse to a small clearing where it could graze, and Anthony sat down on a fallen branch, his hand shaking as he opened the letter. He read quickly, then almost dropped it as he gazed in amazement. What did Isabel mean? What mad scheme was this? He read it again more carefully, and at last stood up and walked slowly over to Will.

'I had a letter which I wrote last night,' he said, 'but I will not hand it to you now. Mistress Isabel has given me some news that needs my consideration. Will you ask her to meet me as she did the other night? Tell her to bring Alice to keep watch.'

'Sir,' Will's face was troubled. 'I said I would pass messages, but meetings—that is even more dangerous. I do not think . . .'

'For a few minutes only,' Anthony urged desperately. 'If you would rather Alice did not put herself in peril, I shall understand, though I would prefer her to be near at hand.'

Will nodded reluctantly. 'Well, this once only, sir. Alice told me that the time before, when you came, Sir Ralph discovered them, though he said nothing to her parents.'

'There is no danger of that this time,' Anthony said quickly. 'He is gone, is he not?'

'Yes, sir, but only for a few days. Alice tells me he will be back when he has finished his business in Kent. Mr Viner, his cousin, is still here.'

Anthony stared at him for a moment, then said firmly, 'It is all the more important that I should see Mistress Isabel. Tell her I shall be there at midnight.'

He stood waiting in the shadows, his eyes fixed on the side door of the dark and silent house. Would Isabel never come? Had Will failed to deliver his message or was she under close guard? Locked in her room, perhaps—unable to escape? He shifted restlessly as the minutes passed until, just as he was beginning to despair, the door opened slowly and in a moment Isabel was in his arms.

She gasped something quickly as he pressed his lips on hers. As he released her, he saw over her shoulder a man standing watching in the doorway.

Isabel felt him stiffen. 'Do not fear, my love. It is Mr Viner. As I told you in my letter, he will help us.'

She turned and beckoned, and Anthony recognised the stranger he had seen in Lady Holstead's withdrawing room.

The two men looked at each other in the moonlight, and Mr Viner smiled gently as he saw the suspicion in Anthony's face.

'I have my reasons for wishing you well in your courtship, sir,' he said softly. 'Will you accept my help?'

Anthony glanced quickly at Isabel, who nodded reassuringly.

'I could not tell you all in my letter, but Mr Viner has promised to befriend us in our need. He has acquaintances in the Netherlands who will shelter us and ask no questions.'

Anthony drew a long breath. 'I thank you, sir, for your offer, but—but—I do not understand.'

'We have no time for explanations now,' Mr Viner said, a trifle impatiently. 'Mistress Isabel will explain all later. You must, however, give me your word that if aught should go wrong you will not betray me to my cousin—Sir Ralph.'

'Your cousin?' Anthony's bewilderment grew. There was a mystery here—something that smacked of treachery. He frowned as he looked at Isabel. Her hood had fallen back, and the moonlight shining on her hair turned it into a golden radiance. Her eyes, under their long dark lashes, were filled with such eagerness that his heart sank. How could she trust this stranger so easily? A man who was disloyal to his own family? A man who, animated probably by some vengeful motive, might well, if it suited his purpose, betray them in the end.

'Listen to my plan,' Mr Viner urged. 'You must be gone in a few days, before my cousin returns. You will go to Dover and stay at an inn, where the landlord—who is known to me—will hide you until a ship is ready to take you as passengers. I shall give Mistress Isabel the addresses necessary and all the information you will need. Have you horses and money, sir?'

Anthony nodded dazedly. 'Enough only to get us over the Channel,' he said reluctantly. 'But, after that, I do not think it would be possible to survive.'

Mr Viner smiled as though satisfied. 'You need have no fear. You would not starve. My friends have important connections. They would obtain employment for you.'

'Well—I must think . . .' Anthony hesitated, then, seeing Isabel's disappointment at his caution, he put his arm round her protectively.

Mr Viner smiled again. 'I shall leave you now, but you must not dally too long. You will have time enough together when you are on board the ship bound for the Netherlands.'

He went quietly back to the house, and Anthony looked down at Isabel. 'I cannot understand why this Mr Viner should be so anxious to help us. Does Sir Ralph know that his cousin bears such enmity towards him?'

'There is no enmity there, but being Sir Ralph's heir, Mr Viner does not wish him to marry.'

'But that is nonsense!' Anthony exclaimed. 'Sir Ralph is young—Mr Viner cannot stop his cousin each time he plans marriage.' He paused, then added apprehensively, 'Isabel—do you not think that perhaps we are being used as pawns in some dark scheme?'

She looked up at him in momentary alarm, then she relaxed, her head against his shoulder.

'No, my love. I think Mr Viner is but taking advantage of the chance that has come his way. He did not know that I would refuse his cousin, but since I have said I am unwilling, he is glad to put off for a little longer a marriage that will disinherit him.'

'Well—I like it not.' Anthony frowned. 'I do not trust the man, and I wish you had not confided in him.'

'I told him nothing,' Isabel drew back indignantly. 'At least, I told him I would not marry his cousin, which pleased him. Then my father told him about you, and later he came to me offering us his assistance. Oh, Anthony!' She slid her arm round his neck and looked up at him imploringly. 'Sir Ralph will return in a few days—my mother is assembling wedding clothes—the priest is coming . . .' She stopped, aghast, and put her hand over her mouth as she felt Anthony stiffen.

'A priest coming to your house? But it is against the law!'

'A man-made law that cannot bind us in conscience,' Isabel said gravely. 'The priest is coming to say Mass. We have often . . .' She hesitated, then went on tremulously, 'I have never spoken of these things even to you, Anthony, but now I must tell you that while he is with us, the priest will be asked to marry me to Sir Ralph.'

Anthony stared down at her in horror. 'A secret wedding! That is what your father meant when he spoke of you leaving your home as Sir Ralph's wife!' He paused. 'But, Isabel, they cannot force you to say the words that give consent.'

'That is true, and though it would be hard, I am sure I have the strength to resist. But it will not be necessary now that Mr Viner has shown us the way to escape. Oh, my love, say that you agree to his plan!'

Anthony's eyes were full of pain as he shook his head.

'Nay . . .' He felt her draw away from him, but he pulled her back fiercely. 'I think it madness. I had already decided that we could not risk our happiness in a foreign country and, although Mr

Viner says he has friends to help us, I cannot find it in my heart to trust him. He would not care what became of us once we were gone. I cannot—I will not—expose you to such danger.'

'But—But . . .' Isabel began to weep softly. 'Then I must suffer here, while you do nothing.'

'That is cruel!' Anthony winced. 'Listen, my love. I think that if you refuse utterly to be married to Sir Ralph, he will withdraw his suit and you will be left in peace. In disgrace maybe, but still unmarried. If we can but wait a little while, the Queen may agree to marry her Catholic prince and then there would be more tolerance in religious matters. When Sir Ralph is gone I will again approach your parents, and together we shall wear down all resistance to our marriage.'

He waited, his heart full of pity as she continued to sob. At last she said, 'And if this does not happen?'

'Well, then, we shall be obliged to flee overseas after all. But I shall have time to make my own plans. Time to write letters abroad so that I can have employment on my arrival. I have given this matter much thought. I think I could be a tutor to some nobleman's children, or a secretary to some landowner or rich merchant.'

'Mr Viner said that his friends . . .' Isabel began, but Anthony shook his head angrily,

'I have said that I do not trust the man.' His voice softened. 'My sweet—You must do as I say. Tell Mr Viner that I cannot accept his offer. Tell him, if you wish, that I am a faint-hearted lover, though God knows it is not true . . .' He bent his head and kissed her fiercely, then quickly released her. 'Have patience, my dearest love, be brave and trust me. Remember that I love you more than my own life.'

Isabel turned away, and for a moment Anthony thought she was going to leave him without a word. Then desperately she flung herself back into his arms and broke into such a passion of weeping that he felt his own heart would break. At last she looked up at him, her eyes swimming, and gently traced the outline of his face with her finger. Then she gave a little sigh and, reaching up, kissed him gently on his lips.

'God be with you, my love,' she whispered. 'I shall do as you wish.'

It was hard to watch her go. Hard to think of what lay ahead for her when the storm broke, but, riding home through the sweet-scented night, Anthony felt sure he had made the right decision. He resolved to tell Will as soon as possible that there was no question of running away, and thus ensure a regular flow of letters. Tomorrow he would sound out Dick Benton and ascertain if he were still on intimate terms with Lady Holstead's maid. Ladies, he knew, were often apt to tell their troubles to the woman who tended them, and knowledge gained in this way might help him to choose the right moment to approach Sir Nicholas.

Three days later, Lady Holstead, cold and distant because of Isabel's refusal to take any interest in the clothes that were being assembled for her future role as Sir Ralph's wife, came to her holding a letter which had been delivered by messenger.

'It is from Sir Ralph,' she announced. 'He comes tomorrow. As he has been fortunate enough to encounter Mr Grant, they will ride together, arriving after dark for greater safety.'

'Mr Grant?' For a moment Isabel looked confused, and her mother tapped her foot impatiently.

'Come, daughter, you cannot have forgotten. Mr Grant will be with us for a week. During that time he will marry you to Sir Ralph.'

Isabel's chin lifted defiantly. 'When the priest asks me if I will have Sir Ralph as my husband, I shall say No.'

Lady Holstead's face darkened.

'I do not think you will bring such shame on your parents, Isabel.' She paused, then added thoughtfully, 'When Mr Grant is here I will arrange for him to have a talk with you. He will soon show you where your duty lies.'

Sitting by the open window in her bedchamber, Isabel gazed out over the garden. Somewhere in the trees a pigeon cooed softly, the murmuring of bees came from the flowers below and all the peace and beauty of the world around her seemed to say that love was the only thing in life that mattered. Sighing heavily, she rose to her feet, then suddenly she caught sight of a man walking past the opening in the tall yew hedge and her heart seemed to stop beating. Surely Sir Ralph would not have returned already? Then, with a gasp of relief, she saw that it was Mr Viner strolling in the garden, and smiled ruefully as she remembered how he had looked at her when she had told him of Anthony's decision. It was a strange look, openly derisive, yet at the back of his scornful smile there seemed to lurk a kind of brooding anger. He had said very little beyond expressing a doubt that she would be able to resist her parents' will for long, then he had bowed and left her. If only, she reflected sadly, Anthony had accepted his offer of help—it would have been far easier to face peril with him than the ordeal she must now endure alone.

Later that evening she handed a letter to Alice. 'Will you pass this on to Will, and ask him to deliver it to Master Anthony tomorrow?'

Alice took it slowly, then looked at Isabel questioningly. 'We have been told that tomorrow evening a priest will arrive and that we may all go to Confession and hear Mass. We have also been told that we must not whisper one word of this to anyone outside the household.' She hesitated. 'Mistress—You have not said aught to Master Anthony of the priest's coming?'

Isabel's eyes blazed in sudden anger. 'You have promised to deliver my messages, Alice, and that is all. Can you not trust me to know what is right?'

Reassured, Alice took the letter away, and Isabel watched from the window as she went off to find Will. It was difficult to avoid feeling guilty at the way she had avoided telling the truth. But Anthony already knew that a priest was coming, and she had told him in her letter only that he would arrive tomorrow. She sighed as she heard voices in the passage outside her room. That would be her mother with the seamstress. In spite of her refusal to show any interest, her clothes were being assembled in piles ready to be packed into trunks and now, she knew, there would be more trying on of the wedding dress chosen for her by her mother. She shrugged. It was useless to resist, so she would continue to stand cold and rigid while they fussed around her. Later, when Mr Grant arrived, she would beseech him to help her and, if that failed, then she would stand mute at the altar.

CHAPTER
FIVE

THE THOUGHT of a papist priest being sheltered in Holstead Hall was still uppermost in Anthony's mind next day. For all his close friendship with the family, he realised now that he not been admitted fully into their confidence. It had never occurred to him that Sir Nicholas and his household ever did more than refuse to take part in Protestant services and pay the resultant fines. That they actually broke the law, and heard Mass while they harboured proscribed priests came as a great shock. He had heard of priests being taken prisoner and executed as traitors but, here in the countryside, such happenings seemed remote from everyday life.

Out in the Mews he stood stroking Jezebel, who sat on his gloved hand, grasping his left forefinger and thumb with one foot and the ball of his thumb with the other, as though she were resting on a comfortable perch. She sat motionless, her yellow eyes alert to every movement around her, and although he usually derived great pleasure from her friendliness his mind was so far away that he stared down at her frowningly.

Suddenly, looking up, he saw that Dick the falconer was watching him curiously, and at last the man spoke. 'Is there aught wrong with Jezebel, sir?

You look mighty concerned.'

'No'—Anthony glanced down at the goshawk, who puffed out her feathers and raised her crest— 'she is in fine fettle, but my mind was exercised on other matters. Tell me, Dick—do you have any dealings with Holstead Hall?'

'Dealings, sir?' the falconer looked wary. 'If you mean with Lady Holstead's tirewoman—I was forbidden by your father to meet her again.'

'Forbidden, yes, but surely you did not find it an easy command to obey?'

A slow flush spread over the other man's face. 'I do not understand you, sir. I am a good servant and do as I am told. I am also a good Protestant and detest all papists.' His eyes narrowed a little. 'We all think alike in this household, do we not, sir?'

Anthony stared. There was something there, a hint of insolence that he did not like. But carefully concealing his irritation, he shrugged lightly. 'We can hate the papist religion, but that is not to say we have to hate the misguided folk who cannot see the virtues of our Protestant faith. Indeed,' he eyed the falconer steadily, 'you must have come to that conclusion when you courted the tirewoman.'

Dick Benton hesitated for a moment, then said slowly, 'I met her first when she was visiting her mother, who lives in the village. We became friendly—she seemed to like me, and she is a comely woman.'

'Then your plans were foiled when the other servants told my father.' Anthony's tone was sympathetic. 'That was a pity, for you might have succeeded in your suit.'

'No, sir.' The falconer spoke harshly. 'I was not seeking a wife. I was seeking information.'

'Information?' Anthony stared at him aghast, but the falconer returned his horrified gaze calmly.

'Yes, sir. It is a papist household, and it is rumoured that traitor priests are always welcome there. The Rector has told us that there is a new law—an Act, he calls it—whereby we ordinary folk can help in the catching of these popish devils and be well paid for our services.'

'God's death!' Anthony looked at the man with loathing, 'A common informer! You would betray our neighbours—who have never harmed you— deliver them up to trial and torture, and all for money. A Judas!'

The falconer's face grew dark with anger. 'No, sir. That I am not! Those papists at Holstead Hall are not my friends. I shall be doing the Lord's work if I am able to put a stop to their superstitious mummery.'

'That is enough!' Anthony turned away in disgust. 'I do not wish to hear such ravings. There is no more I have to say to you.'

'But there is one thing I must tell you, sir. Not as servant to master, but as a fellow Protestant united in religion.' The voice behind him was full of malice, 'I believe that soon Mass will be said at Holstead Hall, and that a travelling priest is on his way there now. What say you to that?'

Anthony wheeled round, hoping that the terror he felt would be taken for astonishment.

'What story is this?' he said scornfully. 'I think you must be mad to believe such rumours. All over the country, folk spread these tales to frighten naughty children. Who told you this fable?'

'Kate Dunn—Lady Holstead's woman,' Dick Benton said sullenly. 'At least, she did not know she was telling me, but when she said that in a few days' time Mistress Isabel would marry their visitor, Sir Ralph Overton, I knew that something was afoot.'

'Fools' talk! Mistress Isabel is not going to be married,' said Anthony firmly. 'So you see that there is no truth is the rumour.'

'But Kate said . . .' the falconer began, and Anthony frowned.

'You had best marry your Kate and turn her into a truthful Protestant,' he said roughly, and hoped that the puzzled look on the man's face meant that he had been put off the scent. To show that all familiarity was at an end, he gave one or two instructions about the treatment needed to keep the birds in good condition while they were waiting for the hawking season to begin in the autumn; then, with Jezebel still sitting on his fist, he walked away.

Usually he enjoyed a stroll round the fields with the goshawk, watching for rats, stoats, squirrels or rabbits. Often Jezebel would see the quarry first and grip his hand suddenly at any movement that attracted her attention. If it was within range, he would slip her at her prey, knowing that she would always return willingly to his hand. But today Anthony's mind was not in tune with that of his pet bird, and soon Jezebel sensed his preoccupation and sat glowering and sulky as he walked aimlessly along.

It was while he was standing moodily looking into the distance that he saw a horseman coming towards him over the brow of the hill, and his face lit up as he recognised Will Rayner. Shortly the groom dismounted and held out a letter.

'From Mistress Isabel, sir.' Seeing the goshawk, he asked, 'Shall I open it for you, sir?'

Anthony assented, his heart racing, then, taking the letter in his free hand, he read it quickly and pushed it into his doublet.

'Will you come back with me so that I can write a reply?' he asked, but Will looked at him apprehensively,

'I fear my absence will be noticed, sir. It would be safer for me to return as quickly as possible.'

Anthony nodded. It was just as well. It would not do for the falconer to catch sight of anyone from Holstead Hall. 'Will you tell Mistress Isabel that she is in my thoughts always,' he said, and after a moment's hesitation added, 'When Sir Ralph leaves, will you yourself let me know in case Mistress Isabel is not at liberty to pass me a message?'

Will stared. 'But, sir . . .' His open countenance betrayed his fear of giving away dangerous information, but then he said, 'Yes, sir. I will let you know.' Lifting his hat, he mounted quickly and rode off.

Anthony stood gazing after him for a long time. So the man did not know the contents of the message he had carried. Pulling out Isabel's letter, he re-read the last lines.

The priest is travelling with Sir Ralph and they will arrive after dark. I should not tell you this, but I know full well that I can trust you.

Of course she could. She knew that he would gladly die rather than harm her or her family. Yet—he frowned deeply as he walked slowly back to the Mews—surely he could make use of this secret information? If the priest could be intercepted and told that his whereabouts was known, he might refuse to enter Holstead Hall and would seek another refuge. London, perhaps, where he could escape his pursuers in the great crowded city. But Isabel said he was travelling with Sir Ralph, who would certainly not be disposed to believe any tale Anthony told him! Besides, that meant the betrayal of Isabel's trust. Oh God! His frown deepened as he replaced Jezebel on her perch and went into the house to rejoin his father.

At table he ate in silence, unaware that Mr Norton was gazing at him speculatively. Suddenly he looked up, as his father said quietly,

'I hear there are visitors at Holstead Hall. Sir Ralph Overton and his cousin. Have you seen aught of them?'

'Yes, sir, I have met them both, but only for a short time.'

'And how is Sir Nicholas? You have not told me how you found him when you visited him on the evening of the storm.'

'He is well recovered from his stay in the Tower, though he was indisposed at first.' Anthony's face flushed at the memory of his humiliation that evening, but his father seemed not to notice anything.

'I think that I shall defer my own visit a little longer,' he said thoughtfully. 'I understand that Sir Ralph and his cousin are both Catholics, so I shall wait until they are gone. It is not always wise to intrude on papist gatherings.'

Anthony stared, his relief mingled with anxiety. Did his father guess that their neighbours were planning to have Mass said in their house? And how did he know that the visitors were Catholics?

'It is strange how speedily news travels,' he remarked lightly. 'No doubt the servants gossip, but I did not think our people held much converse with those at Holstead Hall.'

His father smiled. 'I do not gather my news from servants. Mr Broughton told me.'

'What has the Rector to do with the comings and goings of his recusant neighbours?' Anthony asked uneasily.

Mr Norton shrugged. 'Mr Broughton has been, as you know, easy-going enough, but now he is being prodded by the Puritans, who are on the increase everywhere. They are forever at him to hunt down the Catholics and their priests.'

'But there are no priests in this neighbourhood, nor ever have been.' Anthony said quickly—too quickly, he realised, as he saw his father's eyebrows rise.

'That may well be so.' He shrugged again, and went on calmly, 'However, I do not enquire into such things. I prefer to live in peace with my friends, be they Catholic or Protestant.'

'You are tolerant enough in that respect, sir,' Anthony said a little bitterly. 'But there is something I would like to ask you. Did you know, when you told Dick Benton to put an end to his meetings with Lady Holstead's tirewoman, that he was using her to further his own ends as a spy?'

There was a long silence, until at last Mr Norton said quietly, 'Yes. He told me his reason, but I would have none of it. Why do you ask? Has he disobeyed me?'

'I believe so. I think, too, that he is a dangerous man who would, if he could, betray our neighbours. He is a good falconer, but like all these Puritans he is full of cant and hatred.'

Mr Norton said nothing for a few moments and

sat gazing reflectively at his son. Then he said slowly, 'There is nothing I can do. If Mr Broughton were not so harassed, I would ask him to talk to Dick—though I fear it would have little effect, since the Rector himself is hardening in his attitude towards recusants. Let us hope that Sir Nicholas will not put his family in peril.'

He rose from the table, and his son also rose and bowed as they parted. Outside in the garden Anthony walked around aimlessly, trying to collect his thoughts. It seemed that there was an undertone of meaning in his father's carefully chosen words. Perhaps he was hoping that Anthony would warn Sir Nicholas that this was not the time to take unnecessary risks. He clenched and unclenched his fists. Somehow he must make a plan. Isabel's family must be told that suspicion had fallen on them, and that they were all in danger if a priest were found in their house. He stood still, gazing unseeingly into the distance. Suddenly, it became plain. He would go straight to Sir Nicholas and tell him of his conversation with the falconer. Lady Holstead's maid would have to take the blame for having been so careless in her talk, but that would be no bad thing. It would put them on their guard, and Isabel's trust in him would be justified.

Anthony strode purposefully towards the house, and Mr Norton looked up from his books as his son entered the room.

'I am off to Holstead Hall, sir,' Anthony said firmly. 'I think I should warn Sir Nicholas that folk are watching his movements too closely for comfort. I think too that you, sir, are of a mind with me that this is the right thing to do.'

His father nodded gravely, and said simply, 'I am

glad. I would not have them harmed for the world. But, Anthony . . .' He paused, and looked searchingly at his son. There was something there—a strength of purpose that made him feel uneasy. 'Do nothing rash. Give a friendly warning which may or may not be necessary, but this is all. You must not meddle too closely in papist affairs. Take care, my dear lad.' As Anthony went to the door, Mr Norton added, 'Perhaps, one day, we may all live together amicably, though I do not think that will be for many years—not in my lifetime or even yours.'

The fields were shimmering in the afternoon heat when Anthony set out, and as he came in sight of Holstead Hall he felt a pang of regret for the days that would never return. All the surrounding countryside spoke to him of youthful happiness with Isabel riding beside him, sharing his love of nature and laughing joyously as she raced him over the Downs. He glanced around as though to fix the picture in his mind, and it was then that he caught a glimpse of a familiar figure riding quickly into the small copse he had passed a minute ago. He reined in his horse. That was strange. What was the falconer doing out here at this hour? There could be no reason for his being in this vicinity unless— Anthony drew in his breath sharply—was Dick Benton following him? Spying on his movements, watching to see where he was going? No, that was absurd. The man did not know that Holstead Hall was now forbidden territory, so there was nothing abnormal about the fact that he was heading there as though to visit Mistress Isabel. Nevertheless, Dick Benton was acting strangely. He must have seen his master before he turned into the copse.

Maybe he was stealing off to the village to visit some woman, and did not wish to be seen. Some kind of excuse would be forthcoming, no doubt—an escaped goshawk, perhaps. It was no great matter after all.

A few minutes later he rode into the stable yard, and Will Rayner came forward frowning nervously.

'Sir—It is foolish to come so openly. If someone should see you . . .'

'Never fear, Will!' Anthony smiled grimly as he dismounted. 'I come to see Sir Nicholas himself.' He looked hard at the groom. 'I have a warning for him, and I shall warn you, too.' He paused, his eyes on the other man's astonished face. 'Will—Do you know my Master Falconer?'

Will said stiffly, 'I have met him in company with others, sir, but he is no friend of mine. He is a bigoted Puritan and violent in his views.'

'That is so. Beware of him always. He is likely to become a common informer.'

Will's jaw dropped. Then he said doubtfully, 'But he is your servant, Master Anthony. Why do you tell me this?'

'I have told you because . . .' Anthony hesitated. 'Because, although I am a Protestant, I wish no harm to Catholics. I am for freedom in worship. Be on your guard, and if you see aught that is suspicious, you must warn the household immediately.'

'I understand, sir. But . . .' Will looked at Anthony in dismay. 'I have orders to forbid you entry here. I shall be in trouble if you leave your horse with me.'

Anthony smiled and shook his head. 'There will be no trouble, I promise you. I shall explain all to Sir Nicholas.'

'Very well, sir.' Will watched as Anthony strode round to the house, then, shaking his head in bewilderment, he began to lead the horse away. But before he had time to open the stable door, he saw Anthony coming back.

'Perhaps I had better go in by the side door, as the servants may not permit me to enter.' Anthony grinned ruefully. 'I shall make my way secretly. Think you Sir Nicholas will be in his chamber?'

'I do not know, sir, but Alice is much occupied with Lady Holstead and the seamstress in preparing . . .' He hesitated. 'They are busy with women's affairs, so Sir Nicholas may well be alone.'

Anthony nodded. Even now, he thought wryly, Will would not mention the fact that preparations were being made for Isabel's marriage. Suddenly his new-found confidence faltered. Suppose Sir Nicholas should fly into a rage at the sight of him and refuse to listen to his warning? Well—he drew a long breath and squared his shoulders—a way must somehow be found to make him take heed.

Stealing through the house like an intruder, he found his way to Sir Nicholas's chamber but, to his dismay, the room was empty. He closed the door quickly and continued his stealthy progress to Lady Holstead's withdrawing room. For a moment he listened, and, hearing a low murmur of conversation, drew another long breath and opened the door.

Sir Nicholas and his wife were seated by the open window, gazing out over the garden, and turned astonished faces towards him as he bowed.

His heart racing so hard that he felt almost sick, Anthony said quickly, 'My lady—Sir Nicholas. I have disobeyed you, but I trust you will forgive me.

I bring an urgent warning which I beg you to heed.
You . . .'

He stopped as Sir Nicholas, his face suffused with
anger, rose from his chair.

'Out, sir! How dare you enter my house like a
robber? I shall call my servants and . . .' he looked
angrily down as Lady Holstead pulled at his sleeve.
'No! I shall not listen to this young cub! Go at once,
sir, before my servants throw you out!'

Resolutely, Anthony held his ground. 'You and
your family are in danger, sir. There is talk of a
priest coming here—The villagers are being in-
flamed by Mr Broughton. My father himself wished
me to come and warn you.'

For a moment Sir Nicholas stood speechless, and
Lady Holstead, her face suddenly white, said
quickly,

'Sit down, Anthony, we must hear more.' She
turned to her husband. 'My love, this is no boyish
defiance. Anthony has come as a friend with news
that we are bound to hear. His father has sent him.'

'Ah!' Sir Nicholas subsided unwillingly, and
slowly sat down again. 'Well, I shall hear what Mr
Norton has to say.'

Anthony bowed gratefully to Lady Holstead.
Then, pulling up a joined stool, he sat down.

'My father tells me that Mr Broughton is hardening in his attitude towards you. We have also
discovered that our Master Falconer has gleaned
information from one of your servants—dangerous
information.' He turned to Lady Holstead. 'My
lady, your tirewoman has been a little careless in
her dealings with Dick Benton. He is cunning and
full of malice, and has made her acquaintance in
order to further his own ends.' He paused as Lady

Holstead gasped in horror. 'No, no, my lady, she has not betrayed her trust wilfully, but she mentioned preparations for—for'—he faltered a moment—'a marriage that is planned to take place in a few days' time, and that in itself was enough to arouse her false suitor's suspicion. Master Falconer is as fierce as one of his charges—determined to get his prey—and I fear much damage has been done. Your house will be watched now by hostile eyes, and every visitor will be food for malicious gossip.' He stopped. He must not betray the fact that he knew the priest would arrive that very evening. Carefully choosing his words, he continued, 'I believe that, recently, rewards have been promised to those who become common informers. Dick Benton learnt of this from Mr Broughton, and the thought of being paid for spying has added greatly to his religious fervour.'

He waited. That was as much as he dared to say, and the silence was broken at last by a long, trembling sigh from Lady Holstead as she turned to take her husband's hand.

Sir Nicholas sat motionless in his chair, staring at Anthony as though seeing him for the first time. Then, as he felt his wife's hand on his, he spoke gravely, 'Yes; ah, yes. I understand.' After he had sat in silence again for a while, he said slowly, 'Anthony, you and your father have proved yourselves our true friends. I am sorry indeed that I was violent towards you. We must pray that this fury against us will die down in time. Meanwhile we shall take our precautions and be doubly careful in all that we do.' He thought for a minute. 'Is your falconer still wooing my wife's woman?'

'I do not know, sir. Some time ago my father

forbade him to see her again, but he must have seen her recently to have learnt of the—the marriage plans. She is innocent, I am sure, of any evil intentions, but, gulled by his flattery, she tells more than she should in answer to his cunning questions.'

Lady Holstead smiled a little grimly. 'She will not be so enamoured of him when I have finished with her. She is a good girl, but too trustful. It is hard for servants to understand the vigilance that is necessary.' She shook her head sorrowfully. 'And I fear that I too am to blame. I have treated her as a faithful friend, and I think she is grateful and would sacrifice much for me, but she is still young and unmarried. A man like your falconer may well have bemused her. I must try to find a good Catholic husband for her.'

'And how, my dear,' enquired Sir Nicholas sarcastically, 'will you set about that?' He shook his head. 'No, I think she will have to go. We have no room in this household for foolish women who listen to sweet talk from evil-minded spies.'

'But, sir,' Anthony began nervously. 'Pray do not think me presumptuous, but I fear it would not be safe to cast her off. She will be in despair, and likely to turn to Dick, who would use her as a witness if it should ever come to a trial.' He stopped as he saw Sir Nicholas stiffen suddenly, then plunged on recklessly. 'There may well have been times—I do not know, but I can only suppose— when you have given shelter to priests, and this woman could, under questioning, break down and do you much harm.'

'You are right,' Sir Nicholas said gravely. 'It is easy to obtain information under questioning. Threatened with torture, it needs a strong mind to resist.' He stroked his beard, and saw that Anthony was about to leave. 'Will you thank your good father for his kindness towards us, and assure him that we are most grateful.' He hesitated a moment as though he wished to say more, but the door unexpectedly opened and, to Anthony's great joy, Isabel appeared.

She looked astonished as she took in the scene; then, with a quick glance of defiance at her parents, she flung herself fearlessly into Anthony's arms.

Over her shoulder Anthony saw Lady Holstead put out a restraining hand towards her husband, who was rising angrily from his chair. Seizing his opportunity, he said quickly, 'Have faith, Isabel my love! All may yet be well. It is possible that your marriage will not take place after all.'

He heard Sir Nicholas gasp in anger, but he went on recklessly, forgetting all caution in his desire to comfort Isabel. 'It may be that no priest will come, or, if he does, he will not be here long enough to marry you. I have warned your parents . . .' He stopped abruptly as Sir Nicholas shook off his wife's hand and rose furiously to his feet.

'So this is your game, sir! A pretty plot indeed. You think that by giving us false warnings you will stop a priest coming, and prevent the marriage.'

Angrily he pulled Isabel away and stood facing Anthony, his eyes glaring and his voice trembling with rage. 'You fooled me at first, sir, but now I see through your pretended concern for our safety. A few words of gossip from a servant, and you think to make us tremble and abandon our plans.' Wheeling round, he turned to Isabel.

'To your room, daughter, and pray for grace to overcome your passion for this scheming heretic.'

Dazed and bewildered by this sudden change of front, Anthony found his voice at last. 'But, Sir Nicholas, all that I have said is true. There is real danger, and . . .'

'Danger?' Sir Nicholas stared at him scornfully. 'We Catholics are well acquainted with danger and accustomed to living surrounded by enemies. But enemies who come in the guise of friendship—Ah, God's Body! That is too much! Leave us, master schemer, we do not care for your company!'

His face white, Anthony turned on his heel towards the door. As he passed Isabel, sobbing wildly in her mother's arms, he said, 'Courage, my dear love. I have told you that all will be well.' Then, as Sir Nicholas advanced threateningly towards him, he went out of the room.

Riding home, he reproached himself bitterly for having bungled the whole affair. But what else could he have done, with Isabel in his arms, openly defying her parents? At least, he told himself, he must have sown a seed of warning—enough to put Lady Holstead, if not Sir Nicholas, on guard. She would speak to her woman, who would no doubt break down under her mistress's stern questions. In any case, the danger was still there and even if the priest were admitted to Holstead Hall he would have to face Isabel's mutinous refusal and would not dare to linger in the house waiting for her to weaken in her resolution.

Still deep in thought when he reached home, he walked around to the Mews in search of Dick Benton. A boy working in the yard looked up as he approached.

'Master Falconer be gone into Lewes, sir,' he volunteered. Seeing Anthony's eyebrows rise, he continued importantly, 'He told me he was going to see the magistrates on a grave matter, sir.'

Anthony's heart began to race furiously as he nodded to the boy and turned away. A horrible prospect rose in front of him as he visualised the party of armed men who would ride out and demand entry to Holstead Hall. That would probably be tomorrow for, even if Dick had told them the priest was due to arrive tonight, they would want to trap their quarry while he was saying Mass in the early morning. Well, he must carry out his first plan and try to intercept Sir Ralph and his companion. It would be difficult to convince them, but, somehow, they must be persuaded to go elsewhere. Then the magistrate's men could search to their hearts' content and vent their anger on Dick Benton for having given them false information.

Up in his room Anthony paced about restlessly. He would ride out secretly at dusk, wearing a dark cloak and hat. If anyone should be lurking in the vicinity of Holstead Hall, they would take him for a solitary traveller or, better still, some evil-doer, and avoid speaking to him. Dare he tell his father? No, that would not be wise. He must do this thing alone.

CHAPTER
SIX

CLOUDS CAME up again from the Sussex coast that evening, and a fine drizzle was falling when Anthony set out to take up his vigil. There were several approaches to Holstead Hall but, not knowing which route Sir Ralph would choose, he went as near the house as he dared. Pulling up on the edge of the woods, he endeavoured to calm his thudding heart by thinking of Isabel.

For nearly an hour he waited until at last, with a quiver of excitement, he heard the faint noise of approaching horses. A few moments later, as the sound came closer, his hands tightened on the reins and he drew the mare back into the dark shelter of the trees. Suddenly there was talking and a burst or two of laughter as a party of about a dozen men rode past and pulled up a few yards beyond his hiding-place.

For one fearful moment he thought they had seen him, but a man's voice rang out in the darkness as the leader turned to address the company.

'Put out your lanterns now, and remember, you must not be seen. Surround the house, but place yourselves among trees or against the walls. If anyone approaches, do nothing to prevent their entrance. We must wait until early morning, when the magistrate will arrive. It is then that the papist mummery will begin. The priest will be in his Mass clothes and unable to deny that he is an agent of the Bishop of Rome. Another party will come soon to join you, and you will be well paid if this night's work is successful.'

There was a low murmur of assent and, to Anthony's great relief, they moved on. After a short while he came out of the wood, turned, and rode slowly back along the way he had come, until at last he halted and sat motionless in the saddle, wondering desperately what best to do. It was impossible to go forward, and should Sir Ralph choose another route he would ride straight into the trap prepared for him.

Despair was beginning to envelop him when in the distance he heard a sound that made his blood tingle. Surely that was a horse blowing gently through its nostrils? Straining his ears he listened intently until he was certain, then boldly he rode forward.

With a jingle of harness two horsemen pulled up, and Sir Ralph's voice, calm and untroubled said, 'Good evening, sir. Are you in need of assistance? Have you lost your way on this murky night?'

'Sir Ralph . . .' Anthony said urgently. 'I am Anthony Norton from Vale Court. We met a few days ago when you were out riding with Mistress Isabel.'

'Ah, yes! How do you do, sir? My servant and I are on our way to Holstead Hall. We have been much delayed on our journey. You, too, are out very late.'

Anthony dispensed with formality. 'I have come to warn you,' he said sharply. 'Holstead Hall is surrounded by watchers who will let you in unhindered. But, early in the morning, the magistrate and his men will arrive. They have been given information and are out to catch the priest you call your servant.'

He heard a gasp from the dark figure on the second horse, but Sir Ralph only laughed gently.

'You are a Protestant, I believe, Master Anthony. Are you not yourself interested in hunting down this mythical priest?'

'He is no myth,' Anthony said hotly. 'He is there beside you. When you are in Holstead Hall he will say Mass and then marry you to Mistress Isabel. I know it all, and I wish to save a family I hold dear from the punishment that will follow if this priest is found under their roof.'

Sir Ralph's voice was suddenly hard. 'Why should I believe you, sir? I know full well that you yourself wish to marry Mistress Isabel.'

'That is true, but I swear on my oath that the rest is also true. For God's sake, you must trust me.'

There was a long pause while Anthony prayed desperately for words to convince his listeners. At last the second man broke the silence.

'I believe him, Ralph. Protestant or no, this young man is our friend.' He turned to Anthony. 'I am deeply grateful, sir, that your loyalty to your neighbours has prevailed over your religious principles.' He laughed gently. 'I ought to deplore such an attitude, but in this case I can only be thankful.'

Sir Ralph replied slowly. 'We shall take your word, sir, and pray that God will reward you for your compassion towards us. We had best go back the way we came.'

Anthony heaved a great sigh of relief. 'Where

will you go? I cannot offer you shelter in my house. My father would never . . .'

'No, no. We would not dream of putting you in such peril.' The priest's young voice was warm and friendly. 'We shall find refuge with another Catholic family. Sir Ralph here is my guide.' He added, 'When you next see him, will you explain matters to Sir Nicholas? Tell him to be of good cheer, and in a few months' time, when this alarm has died down, either I or one of my friends will visit him and give his family the consolation of the Sacraments.' He turned his horse's head, 'God be with you, sir. I give you my blessing.'

'Wait!' Sir Ralph's voice was sharp. 'Hark! Can you not hear . . .' He turned to Anthony. 'I think we have been followed. There are horses coming this way.'

For a full minute they stayed motionless; then, with a terrible lurch of his heart, Anthony remembered. 'Dear God!' His voice was a whisper, 'I overheard the leader of a party of men who passed me say that another company would be arriving, but I did not expect them to come from this side of Holstead Hall.'

For another moment he stood staring into the darkness, then quickly made his decision.

'Sir Ralph,' he said quietly. 'You and your friend must hide yourselves as best you can in this small wood and wait while I head these men off. When they are well past, you will be safe to ride back.' He saw their hesitation. 'It is the only way.'

Sir Ralph nodded briefly and the two men disappeared in the shelter of the trees, while Anthony turned his mare's head towards Holstead Hall and sat waiting.

He pulled his hat well down, and as the bobbing lights of the lanterns drew near and began to shine on him he dug his heels into the mare's side. But there were no shouts, no commands to stop his obvious flight, and his heart sank as he remembered the orders the others had been given. Somehow they must be made to chase him, but, with a swift glance behind, he saw that they had halted by the wood. Dear God! A stamp or a whinny from one of the hidden horses, and all would be in vain. Suddenly wheeling round, he galloped back the way he had come and was on them a few seconds later. As they scattered, he rode right through the gap and, bent low over the mare's head, raced on until at last there was a great shout.

'After him! We must take him now, or he will get away!'

He veered off into a narrow pathway as though in panic, then into another side-track, and completing a circle he galloped hard again towards Holstead Hall. Another quick glance and he saw that his pursuers were well past the wood and following him down the rough lane towards the parish church.

It was then, just as he was exulting in the success of his plan, that disaster struck. At full speed, the mare fell into a pothole, and as she came down he was thrown violently forward. There was a moment of blinding pain as his head crashed on the rocky surface of a large boulder. As his pursuers rode up and surrounded him, he gave one groan, and lay still.

In the early hours of the morning Sir Nicholas looked wearily at his wife. 'I do not think Ralph will arrive now, but I shall wait a little longer. You, my dear, should go to your bed.'

Lady Holstead's face was pale and drawn. 'Do you think that he and Mr Grant have been apprehended?' Sir Nicholas shrugged helplessly. 'How can I say? Ever since Will came to tell us that he had seen men approaching this house and then disappearing from sight, I have been dreading that they might walk into a trap. Let us hope that they have got word somehow that suspicion has fallen on us and will not come.' He frowned. 'I must stay awake, for if they should evade these watchers and contrive to enter the house, we shall have to hide Mr Grant at once.' He pulled anxiously at his beard. 'I fear, though, that our hiding-place is not very well disguised. When I was in the Tower, I heard tales of houses being searched, and it was said that panelling beside a chimney-piece is nearly always suspect.'

Lady Holstead shuddered at a vision of pikes being thrust through the tapestries and splitting the woodwork, and got up quickly from her chair.

'The vestments—the altar stone and the crucifix—I must put them in a better hiding-place.' Her lips tightened in an effort to stop them trembling, then she drew a long, firm breath of resolution.

'I shall wear the vestments myself,' she declared, and smiled involuntarily at the shocked expression on her husband's face. 'They will be well hidden under my dress. Or, if I wear my night-clothes, I can cover them with my long cloak.'

Sir Nicholas sighed heavily before he too rose from his chair.

'You speak of night-clothes. It occurs to me

that if, as Will says, there are watchers around this house and they should suddenly demand an entrance, it would look strange if we were fully dressed at this hour.'

'You are right.' Lady Holstead took his arm. 'Oh, my love! What will become of us all?' Her voice trembled momentarily, but Sir Nicholas smiled grimly.

'We shall outwit them yet, my dear. Our cause is just.'

It was nearly dawn when the knocking sounded loudly on the great door.

'Open up in the Queen's name!' The voice below was loud and angry, and after waiting a few moments, Sir Nicholas began fumbling with the lock, grumbling audibly as though disturbed in sleep. At last he flung back the door and, with Lady Holstead standing behind him, faced the group outside.

'This is a fine way to behave,' he said angrily. 'On what pretext do you dare to force your way into a gentleman's house?' He looked at them closely and then addressed himself to a tall man standing at the rear. 'Mr Matthews—I know you, and you know me. What is the meaning of this intrusion?'

The magistrate came forward rather reluctantly. 'Sir Nicholas, we are only doing our duty. We have information that you are sheltering a popish priest, and we must search your house.'

'God's Body! At this hour? A priest? Are you mad, sir, or do you think I am? There is no priest here. What evidence have you?'

The men looked at each other nervously, but the magistrate said firmly, 'We have information, and I have a warrant. That is enough. Stand back, sir, and let my men do their work.'

'If you damage my house, it will go ill with you,' Sir Nicholas roared, but he stood aside as the men poured into the great hall. A few servants roused by the noise attempted to stop them, but were soon brushed aside as the searchers began opening doors and banging on the walls. Sir Nicholas made to follow them, but the magistrate said sharply,

'I must ask you and your lady wife to stay here with me. You too . . .' he signalled to the servants, 'stand over there.'

Lady Holstead, wrapped close in her dark cloak, looked round for a chair and sank into it looking as though she were about to faint. Sir Nicholas took up his stand beside her, holding her hand, while the magistrate stood uneasily at a distance.

Soon the whole house was filled with the noise of tramping feet, violent blows were rained on wood panelling, and angry shouts were heard as servants were disturbed and hustled into the hall to join the others. Oak chests were flung open and their contents thrown on the floor, portraits pulled down, beds torn apart. Pikes were thrust up the chimneys and every locked door was broken open.

Suddenly Lady Holstead, with tears streaming down her cheeks, cried out in alarm as Isabel came running down the stairs with a man chasing after her.

Fear dilated her eyes as she flung herself into her father's arms, and Sir Nicholas shouted to the man,

'Is it part of your foul work to molest innocent women?'

The man was indignant, 'I was not attacking her, sir. I told her to stay in her room, but she ran past me.'

'My daughter will remain here,' Sir Nicholas rounded on the magistrate. 'Finish your devil's work quickly, sir, and get these damned heretics out before they destroy my house utterly.'

'There is no need to abuse my men, Sir Nicholas,' the magistrate protested. 'They are bound to do their duty, and it must be done thoroughly.'

'Bah!' Sir Nicholas almost spat at him. 'You are all dogs, and I shall see that you suffer dearly for this monstrous behaviour.'

Gradually the noise and confusion subsided, and as the men drifted back into the hall, shaking their heads, the magistrate began to look ill at ease. Then, dramatically, a tall figure appeared at the top of the stairs and a man called out triumphantly, 'I think we have him, sir. He says his name is Mr Viner, but that is his story. He admits that he is not a member of this household.'

Mr Matthews rubbed his hands gleefully, and turned sharply as Sir Nicholas gave a great roar of derisive laughter.

'Fools! Mr Viner is my guest. He is a cousin of Sir Ralph Overton, who will be joining us soon from his estate in Kent. If you have not heard of him either, then you are ignorant bumpkins. He stands high in the Queen's favour.'

'I—I . . .' The magistrate stared nervously at Mr Viner, who stood nonchalantly stroking his beard and gazing at him scornfully. 'I must confess that I have not heard of Sir Ralph or of his cousin.' He shifted uneasily from one foot to the other. 'I do not wish to offend an innocent gentleman, but I dare not take your word, Sir Nicholas.' He turned to Mr Viner. 'Can you prove your identity, sir?'

'Why, yes,' Mr Viner said coolly. 'Mr Broughton, your Rector, knows me. I met him the other day when I was out walking. If you care to send one of your men to his house, which is only half a mile from here, he will vouch for me. We had a long conversation, and I found him a very pleasant gentleman in spite of being a poor mis-guided Protestant.'

One of the men laughed involuntarily, and the magistrate flushed. Turning, he gave a quick com-mand, and a man ran swiftly out of the hall.

A silence fell on the company except for an occasional whisper among the servants; then Lady Holstead said quietly,

'Mr Matthews, I would like to go to my bed. I do not feel at all well. Will you allow my daughter to accompany me?'

The magistrate hesitated, then turned to his men.

'Have you searched the ladies' rooms thorough-ly?' At the murmur of assent, he added, 'Two of you men will accompany the ladies and stand guard outside the doors of their bedchambers. There must be no communication between them.'

Alone in her room, Lady Holstead, still wearing the Mass vestments under her cloak, restored the great bed to order, went over to her prie-dieu and sank to her knees. Absorbed in prayer, she stayed until she heard the sound of horses' hooves as the searchers rode away. Then, with a long thankful sigh of relief, she rose to her feet and stood waiting for her husband to come to the room.

After a few minutes she opened the door and

went to the top of the stairs. Gazing down into the hall, she saw Sir Nicholas sitting in his chair. His head was bent, and he presented such a picture of despair that her heart leapt madly in terror.

He looked up as she called out, and as he rose and went to meet her, she saw that his face was drawn and grey.

'My love—what has happened? Did they take Mr Viner after all?'

'No, no.' He shook his head wearily. 'Mr Viner has gone to his bed, but I have tragic news.' He took her arm. 'I shall tell you in your bedchamber. I do not wish Isabel to hear it till later.'

Once upstairs, he drew her gently to the bed. 'Sit down my dear. I do not wish you to faint, but . . .' He hesitated as he tried to think of a way in which he could begin, and Lady Holstead, unable to bear the tension, said sharply,

'It is Sir Ralph—he and the priest have been caught!'

'No. I think they are safe. I must tell you what happened when the man came back from Mr Broughton's house. The Rector, he said, was not there, but a servant had vouched for Mr Viner, and that satisfied the magistrate. Mr Broughton had been called away to Vale Court. My dear . . .' Tears streamed down Sir Nicholas's face. 'Anthony Norton is dead. For some reason which I do not yet understand, he made the searchers think that he was the priest. He rode like a madman, pretending to be a terrified fugitive, and lured them on to follow him. Then his horse fell and he was thrown, hitting his head on a boulder. He died instantly, the men said, and when one of them recognised him, they called the Rector out. Mr Broughton went with the body to Vale Court.' His voice broke. 'That is all I know, and I wish to God I had never lived to hear such news.'

It was a mournful household to which Sir Ralph returned two weeks later, and on hearing the news of Anthony's death he sat, head bowed, in silence. At last he asked quietly, 'What of Mistress Isabel?'

'She spends long hours in her bedchamber.' Lady Holstead looked exhausted and seemed to Sir Ralph to have aged ten years. She sighed. 'It is as though she is willing herself to die.'

There was silence once more, and then Sir Nicholas asked for details of Sir Ralph's journey and the house where he had left Mr Grant.

'He is among friends who are mighty glad to see him,' said Sir Ralph. 'I hope to have him in a few weeks' time at my own house in Kent.' He looked around to make sure they were alone in the room. ''Sir Nicholas—my lady. Do you not think it would be a good thing if you and Mistress Isabel came to stay awhile with me there?'

Lady Holstead glanced quickly at her husband, but said nothing.

Sir Nicholas hesitated, and he looked down at the ground. 'I do not know . . .' His face was troubled, until suddenly he nodded decisively, 'Yes. It might be a wise move. As it is, if we do not go to the parish church within the month I shall have another great fine to pay, but if I am absent from home, it is excused. It seems to me'—he gave a mirthless smile—'that we shall have to spend much time visiting our friends if we are to survive.'

Sir Ralph nodded, and Lady Holstead asked

quietly, 'And what of your plans, sir?'

'My plans?' Sir Ralph looked startled, but quickly relaxed. 'Ah! I understand. My plans for marriage with your daughter.' He looked at Lady Holstead gravely, 'It is my dearest wish to make her my wife, but . . .' He rose and walked to the window, gazing out in silence, while Sir Nicholas and his wife exchanged anxious glances. As he turned to face them, they saw that his eyes were full of sadness. 'I cannot force her to marry me, but I feel strongly that, in time, I could make her happy. One thing, however, troubles me greatly. Do you think she will hate me for being the cause of Anthony's death?'

'The cause? How can you say such a thing!' Sir Nicholas exclaimed. 'You were not to blame for his accident.'

'Not willingly,' Sir Ralph said slowly. 'Nevertheless he sacrificed his life to save us. I know that he did not expect to die, that he thought only of delaying the pursuers long enough for us to escape. He probably hoped that, when he was discovered, he would be able to tell them some tale that would appease their anger. But Mistress Isabel, no doubt, will not look at the matter in that light. I fear she may hate me for the rest of her life.'

Lady Holstead bowed her head, and Sir Ralph asked quietly, 'Has she mentioned my name in her grief?'

His hostess replied, 'At first, when we broke the news to her, she screamed and cried that it was all your fault. I tried to tell her that you too were risking your life by travelling with a priest, but she could see no further than Anthony, so I said no more. Since then, she has hardly spoken.'

Sir Ralph sighed. 'I would dearly love to talk with her, but I think it would only cause her distress. Perhaps in different surroundings . . .' He turned to Sir Nicholas. 'I shall go back to Kent and make preparations for your visit. There is one thing. My cousin Henry—is he still here with you?'

Lady Holstead explained, 'He left two days ago. He said he had changed his mind about building a house in this area, and would look further afield. He asked me to tell you that he may visit you in Kent in a few weeks' time.'

Sir Ralph frowned, and Sir Nicholas glanced at him curiously. 'He is a strange young man, this cousin of yours. He asks rather too many questions about your movements for my liking.'

'What have you told him?' Sir Ralph's voice was sharp.

'Why—nothing. He seemed to be curious as to why you go to France so often, but I reminded him that your mother was French and that her sister is still alive. It was, I told him, very natural that you should visit her from time to time, and that we Catholics must keep on the move in order to avoid paying our fines.'

Sir Ralph nodded, and spoke thoughtfully. 'Sir Nicholas, you know, I think, the real reason for my apparent devotion to my aunt—not but that I am indeed very attached to her—but my other business. Well, that must be kept secret, or our enterprise will fail. Henry's politics are dangerous, and could do our cause much harm.'

'It is not only his politics that could do you harm,' Lady Holstead said gravely, and, ignoring her husband's startled look, added calmly, 'You may put my ideas down to a woman's fears, but Alice, my daughter's maid, has told me of things that my poor Isabel cried out in her grief. Mr Viner, it appears, had offered to help our daughter to flee overseas with Anthony; but, good lad that he was, Anthony did not trust your cousin and refused his offer. Now Isabel is full of bitter regret that the chance was not taken.'

'But—But . . .' Sir Nicholas stared at his wife, his face confused and angry. 'You told me naught of this. Why should Mr Viner plot against his cousin?'

'Why indeed?' Sir Ralph smiled wryly. 'I can think of only one reason. He is my heir if I die without children. Perhaps he hoped to prevent my marriage with Mistress Isabel.'

'I thought that might be so.' Lady Holstead rose to her feet. 'I shall go and tell Isabel that you are here.'

'No—I beseech you . . .' Sir Ralph held out a restraining hand. 'Not yet. It is too soon. When you are ready, come to Kent, and perhaps by then she will look at things differently. I pray that it may be soon.' He paused. 'I would like you to bring her marriage clothes with you. Mr Grant can come to us during your visit . . .' He stopped, and gazed at them questioningly.

'Ah!' Sir Nicholas grew more cheerful. 'That is a good plan. Do you not think so, my dear?'

Tears welled up in Lady Holstead's eyes, and Sir Ralph looked at her compassionately.

'It will be sad for you to lose your daughter, my lady, but I swear to you that I shall be patient and gentle with her. We are both young—there is plenty of time—but we should not waste an opportunity of getting married if a priest is available.

Perhaps, too'—he smiled grimly—'my cousin will be less likely to spy on my movements if he finds he has lost his chance of inheriting my estates.'

CHAPTER
SEVEN

IT WAS not as difficult as Lady Holstead had feared
to persuade Isabel to go to Kent. Still numbed with
grief, she seemed almost to welcome the prospect
of escaping from surroundings that reminded her
constantly of Anthony. She took little interest in
the preparations being made for the journey, but
the hustle and bustle all round her was a distraction, and helped to dull the pain that overwhelmed
her whenever she was alone.

The day before they left she went outside to take
a quiet walk. Already, she noticed sadly, the leaves
on the chestnut trees were beginning to turn gold—
a reminder that autumn was on the way. Autumn,
the season that Anthony had loved so much. The
time when falconry began in earnest. Her heart
contracted as she recalled his face laughing and
aglow after a good morning's sport. No matter
where she looked she could feel his presence and,
desolately, she recalled the details of their last
meeting. If only he had been willing to trust Mr
Viner, they could by now have been starting a new
life together in a foreign country. What comfort
was it that her parents—the servants—everyone—
praised him for his bravery and self-sacrifice? They
would have cursed and blamed him if he had taken
her away, but that would not have mattered when

weighed against the happiness they would have had together. Now there was nothing left for her but sadness and bitter regret. How could she go on living here, feeling his youthful spirit all around, yet knowing that she would never be held in his arms again?

Her eyes burning with unshed tears, she turned abruptly and saw her mother coming towards her. Instinctively she flung herself into the outstretched arms and said wildly, 'Mother, I do not want to go to Kent, but if I stay here, my heart will break!' She looked pitifully into her mother's eyes. 'If Sir Ralph still wishes to marry me, I think I must consent. It is better that way. I cannot go on living here—there are too many memories.

'Oh, Isabel!' Lady Holstead's face lit up. 'You have decided wisely. A good marriage will help you to face life again. Children will be your consolation and help you to forget.'

Isabel drew back. 'I shall never forget Anthony. Sir Ralph must not expect love from me.'

Lady Holstead shrugged gently. 'That will come, my dear child. Even though all seems dark now, one day you will be happy again.'

'I do not think so.' Isabel turned for a moment, gazing at the peaceful garden, her face pale and set, and her mother said no more. Thankful that they would all soon be in fresh surroundings, she went indoors to supervise the travelling arrangements while Isabel resumed her sorrowful walk.

They arrived in Kent a few days later, and as they approached the walls surrounding Overton Place, Sir Nicholas turned to his daughter.

'See, Isabel, is that not a magnificent house? It

was old even in our fathers' time, but from what Sir Ralph has told me it is fine and modern inside. He has made many good changes since his father's death.'

Isabel nodded indifferently, but Lady Holstead said, 'He has replaced all the old horn windows with good glass and put in many fireplaces. Several of those beautiful chimneys are new'—she smiled at her husband—'they were not there when we first visited the family soon after our wedding. I found it mighty cold and draughty then.'

Isabel could not help feeling a sharp twinge of apprehension as they drew nearer to the great house. Built of local stone, it seemed to blend in with the surrounding countryside. Its ancient walls and countless windows glowed mellow and welcoming in the last rays of the setting sun, but to her it spoke only of its owner. Like Sir Ralph, it was awesome and commanding. Sick at heart, she began to regret her hasty decision. How would she ever come to look upon this vast pile as home? Was it here that she must spend the remainder of her life? Suddenly, through a mist of tears, she saw the great gates open and a party of horsemen advance towards them.

Sir Nicholas turned jubilantly to his wife. 'That is just how his father used to come to meet my father when I was a lad. It is a fine way to greet a friend.'

As the two parties met, Sir Ralph at the head of the cavalcade leapt down from a magnificent black stallion and swept off his hat with a great flourish.

'Welcome!' he said gaily. 'A thousand welcomes to you all.' As he looked up from a deep bow, Isabel saw his eyes light up at the sight of her before he turned to her mother and father. After a few words, he came to her and bowed again.

'Mistress Isabel, I am honoured that you should have come so bravely to visit me. I pray that your sadness will be lifted soon.'

He led them into the house, and wine was handed round, while a group of servants emerged from the far end of the hall and stood respectfully in silence. At last Sir Ralph turned towards them and beckoned forward a tall, grey-haired man standing at their head.

'My good Steward, John Fuller,' he said. 'It is he who makes this household run smoothly. He served my parents and will, I hope, continue to assist me for many years yet.'

Isabel caught a shrewd glance as the Steward bowed low, murmuring a quiet greeting, and suddenly, looking at the faces of the assembled servants, she shivered. It was obvious from their expressions that they looked upon her as their future mistress, and her numbed mind began to grasp the enormity of the change that would soon take place in her life. For a moment she felt like turning and fleeing back home, back to all the well-loved familiar places—even back to Anthony's ghost—anything rather than stay here and become the wife of the comparative stranger standing at her side.

The colour drained from her face and, as she swayed, Sir Ralph put out his arm and saved her from falling. Half-fainting, she was conscious of confusion all round her, and then, to her relief, she was helped upstairs to a bedroom where merciful darkness swept over her. When she opened her eyes, her mother and Alice were standing behind her, their faces full of loving concern, which

changed to relief as they saw her return to consciousness.

She began to rise, but her mother pushed her
back gently. 'Sir Ralph has sent word that you must
stay and rest, my love. Alice will help you to
undress and will remain here with you. She has a
small room through there, but she says she will
sleep on the truckle-bed at your feet. Now I must go
and supervise the unpacking of our belongings, and
after we have eaten, I shall come up and say good
night.'

A few minutes later there was a knock at the
door, and a smiling servant entered with food and
drink for two, which Alice took and placed on a
small table.

Isabel turned her face away. 'I cannot eat anything, Alice. You may have my share along with
yours. I wish . . .' She sighed heavily. 'Oh, how I
wish I had never come here!'

'But, Mistress,' Alice looked puzzled, 'it is all so
pleasant. Why, look round this pretty room and see
how everything is provided for your comfort.'

Isabel gazed indifferently around and saw
touches of a luxury to which she had never been
accustomed in her simple bedchamber at Holstead
Hall. Tapestries on the oak-panelled walls, rich
carpets draped over chests and tables, and even one
on the centre of the floor.

Alice followed her mistress's eyes. 'That I have
never seen before!' She looked wonderingly down
at the floor, and then turned to survey the hangings
on the bed. 'These curtains are so beautiful—see
how they match the blue and gold of the ceiling.'

Isabel nodded listlessly. What difference did this
evidence of wealth make to her, when all the time

she was longing for Anthony and the simple life they could have had together? But it was no use repining, she must resign herself to her fate.

Next day, her strength regained, she allowed Alice to dress her in a rich new gown of ivory and black and went downstairs to face the world. Her parents were admiring Sir Ralph's innovations and listening to his plans for future improvements. After greeting her, he made no attempt to draw her into the conversation, but, every now and then, he cast her a quick, compassionate look.

At last he said, 'Come and let me show you the rest of the house. Mistress Isabel, will you care to accompany us, or do you prefer to sit and rest?'

She hesitated for a moment, and replied quietly, 'Thank you, but I am quite recovered. I would like to go with you.'

Lady Holstead looked pleased, and Sir Nicholas said jovially, 'This is a great day for me. I am proud to think that soon my daughter will be mistress of this great house in which there are so many treasures.'

The blood rushed to Isabel's face and, glancing involuntarily at Sir Ralph, she saw a quick flame of triumph in his eyes. Suddenly her whole being was flooded with fierce hatred. He has won the battle, she thought, and thinks that all will now be easy, but I shall never forgive him for being the cause of Anthony's death. He shall learn what it is to have an unloving bride. In place of grief, she found strength in hardness, and made her resolution accordingly. I shall take all these riches, she told herself, but I shall give nothing in return. He has stolen from me all that I valued in life, so I shall have my revenge. If he had not brought the priest that night, Anthony would be alive today.

They went slowly round the house, Sir Ralph explaining the route as they strolled along. They visited the chief living-rooms, were shown the magnificent tapestries, the new panelling, the beautiful furniture and many treasures brought from the Continent, and while her parents praised and admired, Isabel remained coolly indifferent. There was no secret made of the fact that it was, and always had been, a Catholic house. Now and again Sir Ralph moved portraits aside, pressed the panelling and showed them hiding-places he had devised for visiting priests. Many of them led to back staircases or dropped down to the floor below, where other hiding-places led out into the gardens.

'It is full of secret labyrinths,' exclaimed Sir Nicholas, overcome with admiration at such ingenuity.

'I have done my best to prepare for future difficulties,' Sir Ralph said. 'At the moment I am in favour with the Queen's Grace, but it is easy to offend Her Majesty, and I have many enemies at Court.'

Lady Holstead sighed. 'It is a struggle which grows fiercer every day. Sometimes I fear that our cause is doomed.'

'No cause is doomed as long as there are those who are willing to continue the fight,' said Sir Ralph firmly. 'We cannot see the future, but, who knows, the Queen herself may marry her latest suitor. The "Little Frog" is a Catholic.'

Isabel put her hand quickly to her mouth, pressing hard on her lips to stop their trembling. Anthony had used almost the same words, and had counselled patience in the hope that the Royal marriage would be the solution to their problems. But now it was too late, and any cessation of Catholic persecution would only increase her bitterness.

She turned away, conscious that Sir Ralph had seen her distress. Gently, he said, 'Do not look so troubled, Mistress Isabel. There is no more danger to this house. When her Grace heard of the fanatical attack made by the villagers, she was greatly angered and sent a warning to the local justices.'

Sir Nicholas looked thoughtful. 'It is fortunate indeed for you that your father took her side when she was in the Tower. Her Grace is loyal to her friends.'

Sir Ralph nodded, and suddenly, with a longing to hurt him, Isabel said sharply,

'It is a pity that you have to return such kindness by disloyalty on your part, Sir Ralph.'.

'Daughter!' Sir Nicholas turned to her in horror. 'Do you not yet understand that our duty to God comes before all else?'

She paled at his anger, but said nothing, and Lady Holstead hastily distracted her husband by drawing him out of the room and expressing a wish to continue their tour of the house.

Isabel made to follow them, but Sir Ralph took her hand and drew her back. His touch sent a tingle of hatred through her, mingled with a feeling of pleasure that she had offended him, and she met his gaze coldly.

'I think, Mistress, that you and I must settle this question once and for all.' His smile was gently mocking, but there was a glint of anger in his eyes that showed her taunt had gone home. 'I beseech you—nay I command you—to be more discreet in your remarks.'

She shrugged lightly and tried to pull her hand away, but his grip tightened.

'You understand?' His smile had faded and he gazed at her so gravely that her eyes faltered and glanced away. 'There is no disloyalty to the Queen in this house. I am Her Grace's subject, and always shall be. I hold no truck with those who would force her off the throne.'

At last he released her hand and, flushed with fury at his rebuke, she walked quickly after her parents, who were standing at a window looking down at the gardens. As Lady Holstead expressed her admiration, Sir Ralph suggested that they should take a turn outside, and led them into the sunshine.

In spite of herself Isabel began to enjoy the leisured stroll down the yew walk and the beauty of the Italian garden. They stood for a while looking back at the house, and Sir Nicholas discussed the armorial coats on the tall oriel window of the great hall. 'I look forward to seeing that blank pane filled with my family's crest mingled with yours,' he said.

'I, too, look forward to that day,' Sir Ralph smiled. 'I only wish my father could have lived to see it.'

'God rest his soul, and that of your lady mother,' said Sir Nicholas piously. 'It is sad that they will not see their grandchildren.' Then he said cheerfully to his wife, 'We are more fortunate than they, are we not, my dear? Perhaps, in a year or two . . .' He stopped as he saw Isabel walking away. Catching sight of his wife's frown, he shrugged and grinned at

Sir Ralph. 'The maid is over-modest, I fancy, but time will cure that, or you are not the man I think you are.'

Sir Ralph made no comment, but led the party to look at the stables and kennels. There was so much to see that eventually Lady Holstead sank down on a bench in the elaborately laid out south garden, declaring that she could go no further until she had rested. Her husband placed himself by her side, and Sir Ralph turned to Isabel.

'If you are not too tired, Mistress, I would like to show you one thing more. It is just beyond this hedge.'

Reluctantly she allowed herself to be led into the little orchard garden, and Sir Ralph said gently, 'In truth there is nothing spectacular here. It was a small subterfuge on my part. I wish to talk to you privately. Let us sit here out of earshot of your parents.'

She sat down resignedly, spreading her skirts as wide as possible and folding her hands in her lap. He seated himself beside her, and there was silence for a few minutes until he murmured, 'Do you hate me, Mistress?'

'I—I . . .' She stopped. If he guessed how she felt towards him, he must know that she held him responsible for Anthony's death. She pulled herself together and looked at him steadily.

'How can I do other than hate you, when you have killed the only man I shall ever love?'

He frowned. 'Why do you consent to marry me if you dislike me so much?'

'It will make my parents happy,' she said coldly. 'As for me—it is the only way I can escape from surroundings that will always fill me with sadness,

and bitter regret that Anthony and I did not . . .'
Once more she stopped, as she saw the dark eyes
narrow in sudden understanding.

'You did not . . .? Did not run away together?'

'Yes.' She had only one desire now, and that was
to hurt him as much as he had hurt her. 'We could
have been in the Netherlands, but for you and your
priest. Mr Viner promised . . .' She faltered as he
stiffened and stared at her, suddenly alert.

'Henry? What did he promise you?' Sir Ralph
spoke softly, but his voice was cold and his eyes
hard. 'Where does my cousin come into this tale of
young love?'

'I cannot say—you must not press me . . .' Dis-
traught at having betrayed Henry Viner's confidence, she began to tremble violently.

Rising to his feet, he stood looking down at her,
drawing his dark brows together, and strode away.
For an instant, she thought he had left her. Almost
immediately, however, he returned. 'Your parents
have gone indoors, so we shall not be interrupted.
Continue, if you please . . . I have already been
told of this conspiracy, but I wish to hear it from
you.'

'No.' She stood up and faced him defiantly. 'I
have said too much. It is of no importance—it is all
over, and I cannot talk about it.'

'Oh yes, you can, my beautiful Mistress. You
shall not leave here until you have told me what I
wish to know.'

Defeated, she sank down again on the bench. 'It
is little enough,' she said scornfully. 'Mr Viner
offered to help us to flee to the Continent. He told
me he wished to stop your marriage on the grounds
that, if you have no heir, he will inherit your estate.

Unhappily, Anthony did not trust him and would not accept his offer.'

Her eyes clouded as she relived that last fateful meeting, and Sir Ralph gazed at her for a few moments in silence. At last he said, 'And what form did my cousin's offer take? How was he going to assist you?'

She dragged her thoughts away from the past. 'He told us to go to an inn on the coast, where we would be sheltered until a ship was ready to take us across the Channel. Then we were to stay with friends of his who would find Anthony a post so that we could live in reasonable comfort.'

'How very unfortunate for him that Anthony did not trust him,' said Sir Ralph drily, 'and how very wise of Anthony. You would have been abandoned once you were out of the way. Well, since Henry's plans came to nothing, I shall not tell him what you have told me, but it will put me on my guard for the future. He will come here to visit us after our wedding, and I . . .'

'Our wedding?' Isabel looked up at him, her eyes wide with fear. She knew it had to come, but to hear it spoken of with such certainty filled her with terror. In a sudden wild desire to escape, she said quickly, 'But surely you will not wish to marry me now? You said once that you did not want an unwilling bride.'

As though he had not heard her, he continued, 'I have one more question. How was it that Master Anthony knew of the priest's arrival that night? Did you tell him?

She flushed guiltily. 'Will Rayner, our servant, told us afterwards that there had been talk of the Master Falconer at Vale Court. Anthony had warned Will that this Dick Benton was a spy, so it might have been from him that Anthony heard.'

'And you yourself? You did not tell Anthony?'

Unable to prevaricate any longer, she nodded unhappily. 'I sent him a note. But I knew I could trust him.'

He nodded grimly but said nothing, and his very silence caused her face to whiten. Frantically she jumped to her feet.

'No, no! That is too cruel! You are telling me that *I* sent him to his death!' She stared at Sir Ralph so piteously that his stern eyes softened.

'You must not believe that.' He took her gently in his arms and, all hatred forgotten for the moment, she did not resist. 'I am sure that Anthony learnt enough from the falconer. He would have waited every evening until we arrived. But this I must say . . .' He put his hand under her chin and looked gravely into her tear-filled eyes. 'You must never again tell anyone of a priest's movements. Do not take this as a condemnation—it is merely a warning to be more discreet in future.'

Suddenly his mouth came down on hers in a kiss that weakened all her resistance. Dimly she found herself responding, almost—the thought crossed her mind in a flash—almost as though she were kissing Anthony. Anthony! His name shot through the thrill of physical pleasure and, bitterly ashamed, she fought wildly against the overwhelming strength of the arms holding her prisoner.

'Do not struggle so, my love. This is the way to happiness.' The laughter in Sir Ralph's voice roused her to fury.

'Let me go, sir! I am not your love nor ever shall be. You have no right to treat me so.'

'For the moment that is true,' he agreed and let her go. His smile vanished as he saw her flushed and scornful face. 'Remember, though, that you have consented to marry me. Or have you changed your mind again?'

Isabel smoothed down her dress and put her hands up to the loose tendrils of hair falling about her face. Was this an opportunity for her to escape? Should she tell her parents that she was resolved to return home with them? But what then? There would be other suitors—she would be under constant pressure to marry someone, and Anthony's presence would haunt her until she eventually capitulated. She drew a long breath and said, half to herself, 'If there were any convents left in England, I would gladly enter one, but . . .'

He burst out laughing. 'A convent—you? Mistress Isabel, I do not think you have a religious vocation. You may not love me with your heart, but your body is ready and willing to give itself up to joys that only a lover can arouse.'

She flushed scarlet, but suddenly he frowned, 'There is probably a good reason for your consenting to marry me, in spite of your ill-concealed hatred. I am, of course, very rich.'

She returned his mocking gaze with a scornful look, refusing to be humiliated by his suggestion.

'I had not considered your riches, sir, but, as you say, it is a good reason for marrying without love. You will no doubt be an excellent Catholic son-in-law to my father, paying his fines and saving him from selling his land, which will, in the end, be to your advantage.'

His mouth twitched in amusement. 'I can see that we are going to have an interesting life together.

You will certainly add spice to my hitherto dull existence.'

She turned away and began to walk towards the house, but he called her back.

'One moment more, please, Mistress Isabel. There is something I must ask you.'

She waited, and as he came up to her, he said, 'Next week, God willing, a priest will come to this house and stay for several days. Before he leaves to continue his journey, I would like to ask him to marry us. Is that agreeable to you, Mistress?'

'So soon?' Her mouth trembled, and then she drew a long breath and looked at him steadily. 'It shall be as you wish.'

During the hurried preparations for her marriage, Isabel seemed to be in a trance, enduring submissively the many fittings of still more new gowns, her mother's anxious glances and the excitement of the entire household, until at last she stood, pale and grave, at the altar.

She looked, Alice had told her, like a golden lily in her pale primrose damask dress, with a gold bejewelled girdle clasping her slender waist, the bodice patterned with creamy pearls and a coif of pearls on her long flowing hair.

The room was filled with the fragrance of newly-strewn herbs and flower petals, and the altar was banked high with roses and lilies. Sir Ralph, beside her, was magnificent in rose-coloured velvet ablaze with sparkling jewels, but to Isabel he was as unreal as a ghost, as also was the young priest who was gazing at her so seriously.

Even in her numbed state, Isabel had been impressed by the priest's quiet manner, and in some vague fashion he seemed to give her strength. If that brave young man could face his dark future with such calm courage, she too must accept her fate with equanimity.

It was only when she lay in the huge bed in the marriage chamber, waiting for Sir Ralph, that panic swept over her. Her thoughts flew to Anthony, and she began to weep bitterly. How joyous she would have been had it been him for whom she was waiting. Not here in this great bed with its gorgeous hangings, its silken sheets and down pillows—she would not have cared if they had had to share a rough pallet in some dingy foreign hovel. Burying her face in the pillow, she sobbed his name repeatedly in utter despair.

Absorbed in her grief, she did not hear the door open as Sir Ralph came quietly into the room and stood looking down at her. For a few minutes he listened grimly, then, bending down, he touched her on the shoulder. She whirled round in terror and shrank back, staring at him through her tears.

'Madam . . .' His voice was cold. 'I did not expect a loving welcome, but I do not care to hear you calling another man's name in our marriage bed. You must forget the past, and remember to be faithful to your vows even in your thoughts.'

Slowly he went round to the other side of the bed and flung aside the covers. 'Now dry your tears,' he commanded, 'and come to my arms.'

He was very gentle with her, but she was so rigid in her terror that at last he was forced to take her in a blaze of passion. She cried out in pain, and remorsefully he tried to comfort her, but as soon as she was free she turned away, her whole body trembling in revulsion.

'Sweetheart,' he said gently. 'You should not have been so resistant. I promise you it will not be like this again. Sleep now for a while. Later I will teach you how to find pleasure in our union.' He paused. 'Will you try to give yourself to me willingly?'

He waited in the darkness for her reply, but, still shuddering violently, she said nothing. At last he said grimly, 'Very well. I shall not touch you again tonight. Indeed, I shall leave you alone until you offer yourself to me of your own free will.' Turning on his side, he went to sleep.

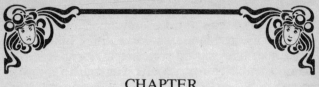

CHAPTER
EIGHT

A FEW WEEKS later Sir Nicholas and his wife left Overton Place, and although Isabel wept at their departure, she was comforted by the fact that Alice had consented to remain with her for a few months until such time as Will would come to fetch her and take her back in time for their proposed marriage in the spring. Mingled with Isabel's sadness was a secret feeling of relief, for ever since her wedding night, it had been difficult for her to talk with her mother. Lady Holstead was plainly hoping to be taken into her daughter's confidence, and her probing questions made Isabel nervous and withdrawn. How could she explain that Sir Ralph had not been near her since that first night? He slept in an adjoining room and although he treated her with the utmost courtesy on the few occasions when she was alone with him, he had become an unapproachable stranger.

An hour or two after her parents' departure, however, her secret feeling of relief changed to a longing to follow them—to cast herself on her father's mercy and beg to be allowed to return home and resume her former way of life. Wandering desolately in the garden, she made no effort to stem her tears and eventually sank on to a bench, weeping bitterly. At last, exhausted, she dried her eyes and rose to her feet. The air was warm on this calm, golden day in late September, and looking back at the old house she was struck by its magnificence. She was, she reflected, surrounded by beauty and all the comforts that wealth and privilege could bring. Instead of weeping over the past, she would accept her situation and bury her sorrows in a new life. Deep in her thoughts, she scarcely noticed the sudden barking of dogs and the sound of voices, until suddenly she saw her husband in the distance with his two favourite spaniels at his heels. Her heart began to pound, but, filled with her new resolve, she drew a long breath and stood waiting calmly as he approached. The dogs jumped around her and she bent to caress them. Looking up, her face flushed and her eyes smiling at their antics, she met Sir Ralph's astonished gaze.

'I had thought to find you weeping, madam, and came to condole with you on the departure of your parents, but I see . . .' He looked at her more searchingly. 'Ah! There have been tears, but now you are recovered. You are resigned, I trust, to your dreadful fate as mistress of this establishment?'

'That, sir, is what I have been telling myself, and since there is no escape, I must needs do my duty.'

He winced involuntarily. 'You were not forced into this marriage, madam. You came to me of your own expressed wish.'

Her flush deepened, and she looked away. Pulling a cluster of leaves from a lavender bush at her feet, she crushed them in her fingers and bent to smell them. But their sweet fragrance brought back memories of the bushes under the windows in her old home and, fearful of weeping again, she cast the leaves aside. Glancing up, she forced herself to look Sir Ralph steadily in the face.

Still in his riding-clothes, his leather gloves held lightly in his hand, he stood, tall, handsome and forbidding, with his gaze fixed on her. 'I know full well why you married me,' he said gently. 'You turned to me as a refuge—an escape from sad memories. I know also that you do not love me, and I shall not force myself upon you while you are pining for your lost happiness. One day I hope you will come to me of your own free will.'

She met his eyes bravely. 'I shall not go back on my side of the bargain. You have given me all this'—she turned to gaze round her—'and I am ready to pay the price.'

'God's Body, madam!' Suddenly he lost patience. 'You speak like a whore who sells herself to the highest bidder! Did you come to me for riches alone?''

She turned away, but he took her arm in a hard grip and pulled her round to face him. Shivering at the burning fury in his eyes, she stammered, 'No, no. I did not mean . . .' Then words failed her. In a sense, he was right. She had indeed turned to him for refuge, but his wealth and possessions had certainly influenced her decision. Standing stiff and cold in his grip, she said evenly, 'I married you because there was no one else, and because I knew my parents would be pleased.'

His eyes were still full of anger, but he nodded as though he accepted her explanation. 'No one else—Yes, that is true, and no compliment to me. Nor will there ever be anyone else. It may be that you will meet many men in our life together but, let me warn you, madam, I am not to be trifled with.

You will find me a jealous husband.'

'Other men . . .!' She stared at him. 'You talk to me of other men! I who have known true love—the love that comes but once in a lifetime.' She paused, suddenly desolate, and added slowly, 'I shall never love again.'

He let her go and stood for a few minutes in silence. Then he spoke softly, his anger gone and his voice full of pity. 'Isabel, my sweet wife, life is long and you are young. For your comfort I must say one thing. There are two kinds of love. The first is ardent and consuming and sometimes it lasts, but more often it dies and is replaced by another love that is deep and true and lasts a lifetime. I speak from experience. I, too, loved a woman once, as you loved your Anthony, but it came to nought and I thought my heart was broken.'

Isabel saw that his face suddenly looked pale and drawn. She felt a strange, quick pang in her heart. In spite of the fact that he spoke of his lost love in the past tense, it seemed that he still cared. The thought should have comforted her, sharing as they did a grief in common, but instead she felt more desolate than ever. In his own words he had strengthened her conviction that he had married solely to do his duty to his dead father. He was, it appeared, only acting the part of a loving husband, when in reality . . . Hastily she pulled herself together as he began to speak again.

'I have news for you, madam. I am obliged to go to London, and must leave you here alone for a short time.'

Taken by surprise, she said indignantly, 'You would leave me here—your newly married wife? Are you ashamed to have me meet your friends? Is this then to be my life, always to be kept in your country home, never to go to London—to the Court—to . . .'

She stopped, overwhelmed by the vision she had conjured up of a neglected wife kept hidden away, unloved and necessary to her husband only as the future mother of his children.

He frowned as though he read her thoughts. 'There are times, madam, when I shall be only too pleased for you to accompany me, but on this occasion it is not possible. My business is with the Queen. I have to plead with her, and it would not help my cause if I were to have a young and beautiful wife at my side. Her Grace does not take kindly to the marriages of the men who pay her court.'

'You have to plead with her? Why? Are you out of favour with her because you have married me?'

He smiled wryly. 'No. I have not yet told her. But the favour I ask may well anger her. I go to plead for the life of Edmund Campion, the Jesuit priest.' He saw the look of alarm on her face, and added, 'Let us walk here awhile, and I shall explain what I have to do.'

He told her then, as they strolled in the warm sunshine, that having evaded capture for nearly a year, Campion had at last been caught, along with several other priests. He was charged with treason and still awaiting trial. It was known that he was already being tortured to force information from him as to the whereabouts of other priests in England and also to make him confess that he was plotting to rouse the country against the Queen.

'They will never allow that Campion's reason for being in this country is solely a religious one. The

Queen herself does not like it to be thought that she persecutes her Catholic subjects. She professes tolerance for all religions, so a charge of treason must be built up in order to justify the execution of all priests who come to minister to their people.'

'But why you? Why should you plead for Campion? It is bound to put you out of favour with the Queen. Are there not others in higher places with more influence? And, if not, what hope have you of success?'

'It is my duty,' he said evenly. 'Her Grace has vowed that she will never forget the help my father gave her when she was a prisoner in the Tower, so I must hope that she will listen to me favourably. I have never yet asked her for anything, so perhaps—well—I must at least try to use what small influence I possess.'

He felt silent, and when at last he spoke again it was to tell her that she need not trouble herself in any way with the running of the household. That would be in the capable hands of John Fuller, the Steward. Then he bowed and said quietly, 'I shall ride at dawn, madam. I hope to return within a week.'

The week passed for Isabel like a strange dream. In spite of the fact that she was surrounded by servants all anxious to please, she would have felt lonely indeed in the vast house had it not been for Alice and Mr Fuller. The Steward, deferential yet fatherly and kind, filled the days with interest by showing her the workings of the great establishment of which she was now the mistress. He was, it was plain to see, devoted to Sir Ralph, and occasionally let fall such praise of his master that she found it difficult to reconcile her own view of her husband with that of the man who had known him since childhood.

On the evening of the day when Sir Ralph was expected to return, Isabel retired to bed early. Vague fears had been forming in her mind, but now that a head cold had declared itself she hoped that this was why she had been feeling unwell for the last few days.

She was unable to sleep, however, and when at last she heard noises below that indicated Sir Ralph's arrival, she pulled on a bed-gown and sat waiting by the fire. It gave a welcome warmth in the chill of the autumn evening, but nevertheless she shivered when the door opened.

Rising to her feet, she curtsied, her beautiful hair, unbound, falling round her face. 'I am pleased to see you, sir,' she said coolly. 'My excuse for not greeting you sooner is that I have a small head cold. How was it with the Queen? Did you see her?'

He walked over to the fire, where he stood gazing down at the flames. At last he turned. 'My mission failed, madam. Her Grace was greatly enraged by what she termed my audacity.'

Alarmed at his sombre look, her face turned pale and she clasped the bed-pole as though she felt faint. He stared at her in surprise.

'I did not think to find you so concerned over Father Campion, madam. Ah!'—his eyes narrowed—'It is not the priest's fate that troubles you—you fear the Queen's displeasure.' He shrugged scornfully, but almost immediately his expression changed to one of concern as, deathly white, Isabel slid to the floor.

In one stride, he bent over her, gathered her up

and laid her on the bed, where she stayed with eyes closed for a full minute. At last her lids fluttered, and she murmured something indistinct.

'I shall call your maids,' he said anxiously. 'I did not know you were so ill.'

'I am not ill'—her voice trembled—'I think . . . I do not know—it is too early, but . . .' She gazed at him in confusion, as he stared back at her in sudden comprehension.

'By Our Lady!' he said softly, and lifting her in his arms he held her tightly against his heart. 'One night only—a sad one, too, for us both, and yet God has blessed our union already.'

Putting his hand under her chin he bent to kiss her, but she stiffened and drew back quickly.

His face grew dark as he saw the bitterness in her eyes. 'By God!' he said harshly. 'You hate me for it!'

Releasing her at once, he let her sink back on the pillows and, turning on his heel, went to the door to call for her women. Then he came back and said coldly, 'I wish to be informed of your progress, madam. Take care that you do nothing foolish. I trust you will feel better in the morning.'

In spite of a restless night, Isabel did indeed feel much better next day and, ignoring Alice's anxiety, refused to stay in bed.

''Tis but a cold,' she said impatiently. 'I shall wear my blue velvet gown—that will be sufficient to keep me warm. Come, dress my hair. I am eager to hear more of Sir Ralph's news.'

'Mr Viner has travelled back with him, my lady.' Alice picked up the comb. 'He told Mr Fuller that they met in London.' She said slowly, 'Will it not seem strange to see that gentleman again?'

'Mr Viner?' Isabel stared at Alice in the mirror, then suddenly her face grew pale, 'Oh, but you are right! To see him again will bring back such sad memories.'

'My lady, things are different now. You may be sure he will not talk of the past.' Alice paused, then added compassionately, 'If you wish, I shall send word that you are not well enough to leave your bedchamber.'

'No, Alice. I shall not be so foolish. I cannot always avoid him. I must not let his presence agitate me.'

When eventually she descended the great staircase, she had assumed a calm, seemingly confident manner that caused Henry Viner's eyes to widen in admiration as he bowed over her hand. All too conscious of Sir Ralph's steady gaze, she suggested that they should take wine in the small parlour, and when they were seated, she said coolly, 'Mr Viner has no doubt already heard your news, sir, but will you not tell it again so that I may learn what occurred?'

Sir Ralph took a few sips of wine, and said slowly, 'It is not a happy tale, madam. At first I told the Queen that I was newly married, and Her Grace did not care for that. She asked if I had had the good sense to marry a Protestant, and looked at me grimly when I said you were Sir Nicholas Holstead's daughter. After a while she seemed to relent, so then I presented my petition. I went on my knees and asked very humbly if she would release Edmund Campion and allow him to go into exile in France.'

His mouth twisted, and he stared ahead as

though reliving the scene. Shaking his head, he continued ruefully, 'Her Grace enraged is like a tiger. She half rose in her chair, and I thought she would strike me, but she sank back and sat glaring at me furiously. At last, breathing hard in anger, she said sharply that she had seen Campion recently and had offered him his freedom if he would but conform to the Protestant religion. Then, suddenly, she shouted, "He threw my merciful offer back in my face and for that he must suffer the proper punishment!"' Sir Ralph sighed deeply.

'I saw then that my cause was hopeless, yet I tried one desperate last appeal. I implored her to show compassion in view of the tortures Campion had already endured, but that was too much for her. She swore at me and shrieked that, if it were not that my father had befriended her in the Tower, she would send me there to join my fellow papists. Finally she told me to be gone from her sight and never to show my face at Court again.' Sir Ralph rose abruptly and went to the window, where he stood staring out into the garden.

Isabel sat speechless with horror, and it was Henry Viner who broke the long silence.

'As I said when you first told me this sad story, Ralph, it was a fruitless errand, and one that has done you great harm. You have increased the danger to your household, and we shall all be suspect now.' He shrugged. 'Well I, for one, shall now appear to conform with the new religion—for a while, at least.'

'Cousin!' Sir Ralph wheeled round and stared at Henry in disgust. 'You cannot be serious!'

Henry Viner shrugged. 'I have little choice in the matter. I become poorer every day. Last year I was obliged to sell my house in London; with the money, I had hoped to buy a small estate in the country, but with these ruinous fines I find even that is impossible.' He sat gloomily contemplating his glass. 'I had also thought that perhaps you would be able to use your influence to help me to obtain a post at Court, but now it is apparent that my application would not be considered favourably.'

Sir Ralph smiled wryly. 'So it will be upon my conscience if you turn Protestant?'

'In part.' Catching sight of the scorn in his cousin's eyes, Henry said angrily, 'It is easy for you to condemn, but I see no other way. I suppose I could go abroad—I have friends in the Nether-lands—but it would mean taking a humble post as tutor or something equally menial. Now, France'— he glanced calculatingly at Sir Ralph's stern face— 'that is a country more to my liking, but I know no one there of any importance.'

Isabel, listening gravely, felt that her sympathies lay with Henry, yet, gazing at him searchingly, she sensed that his words held more than an attempt at self-justification. There was an undercurrent of tension, a hint somewhere of dangers ahead, and glancing at her husband, she saw that his eyes had become coldly alert.

Henry spoke again. 'I was wondering, Cousin. Your aunt in France—she lives, I understand, in great state. Do you think you could give me a letter of introduction to her? Maybe she could find a post for me in her household or perhaps in that of some other noble house? What say you to that?'

'Ah, there you are wrong.' Sir Ralph shook his head. 'You would not, I am afraid, be welcome.

She does not care for the English. I myself, being her nephew, am accepted because I am half French and the son of her favourite sister.' His mouth curled a little grimly. 'She is also a staunch Catholic. I fear your lack of fervour would soon be perceived.'

Henry laughed. 'That would present no difficulty to me. I can be fervent enough if I am no longer in danger. Surely she would look kindly on a poor persecuted Catholic obliged to flee his country for conscience sake?'

'I do not like hypocrisy, Cousin,' Sir Ralph said coldly, 'and I have told you—my aunt cannot abide the English.'

'Ah!' Henry sat back in his chair and pulled at his beard thoughtfully. Glancing across at Isabel, he said maliciously,

'My lady, you will have to brace yourself to meet a frosty reception when you go to France with Ralph. It seems that this fierce dame will be displeased at her nephew's choice of an English bride.'

Isabel stared. 'I?—I go to France?' She turned to search her husband's face, and saw a quick frown.

'Henry, you have spoiled the surprise I was keeping for my lady.' He smiled across at her. 'I shall tell you more later, but first I must put poor Henry's mind at rest.'

Sir Ralph's face grew serious as he turned to his cousin. 'I, as you remind me, am rich. It would therefore be unjust if I did not help you, and this I shall most certainly do. I shall pay your fines and, in addition'—he paused—'there is a small manor house and land in Dorset which belongs to me.' He rose, and bowed to Isabel. 'Pray excuse me, madam. We shall leave you for a while to discuss this property. Come with me, Henry. There are documents to be studied.'

Isabel sat alone in the quiet room, her mind filled with excitement. The talk of going abroad was so unexpected that she found it hard to believe. Somehow she had never thought of Sir Ralph as half-French, with relations across the Channel. Even the hint dropped by Henry Viner that she might not be kindly received did not disturb her overmuch. The prospect of travelling to France was so wonderful that briefly she forgot all the unhappiness that she had experienced in the past few months. Life was beckoning to her, showing her that the future might not be as dark as she had imagined.

In an effort to calm herself, she picked up her embroidery and settled down by the window, drawing the coloured silk through in an intricate design that nevertheless failed to put her mind at rest.

At last the door opened, and Sir Ralph said, 'Henry is in the Long Gallery. Will you join us, madam? We shall have no other exercise today in view of this rain.'

Folding her needlework, she rose to her feet, and then, as he offered her his arm, said, 'I trust you will give me fair notice before we go to France, sir. There will be much to prepare—my clothes—I shall need your advice. I have never before made so long a journey.'

'I do not yet know the day, so you will be wise to begin your preparations as soon as possible in order to be ready at short notice.' He paused as they reached the door, then looked down at her, adding, 'I wonder, though, if you will be well enough to stand the journey. If your hopes should be realised, then it might not be wise for you to travel at this time of year. The autumn gales are sometimes severe.'

'My hopes?' Her eyes flashed. 'Not mine, Sir Ralph! I have no desire to bear your child.' Sick with disappointment, she pulled her arm away. 'I have no wish to walk in the Gallery, sir. I prefer solitude to your company.'

Reaching out, he grasped her by the shoulders and forced her to look at him, and she saw that his face was white and drawn. 'Will you never stop hating me, Isabel?'

She shook her head mutely, already regretting her impulsive outburst but too proud to withdraw her bitter words. Eventually he said, 'It must be that I am repulsive to you. Well, we are married, and there can be no question of breaking such a sacred bond, but it seems that I must seek my comfort elsewhere.'

He made a deep bow and went out of the room, leaving her trembling and frightened at his icy manner. She wanted desperately to call him back, but it was too late. Slowly she walked over to the window and stared out at the leaden sky. Her head was awhirl with confusion. She had shown him her real feelings, made it plain that she hated him, so why now did she feel so desolate? Had she spoken the truth? Was it really hatred that made her shiver inwardly at his touch? Hatred that made her heart leap whenever he entered a room? Hatred, or—or the beginning of love? Not the love she had felt for Anthony—that sweet first dawning of a young, unawakened girl—but something stronger, deeper. Some inward yearning that held in it more passion than she could ever have believed possible. She recalled her wedding night, and her face grew hot

with shame as she remembered her rejection of his
gentleness. Pacing blindly up and down the room,
she realised that she could no longer deceive herself. It was indeed love, and she had thrown it
away. It would never be returned, for he had said
that he would seek consolation elsewhere; that he
could say it so callously was a sure indication that he
had never really cared deeply for her. Searching
her memory, she could not recall him ever having
said that he loved her. Now, what little affection he
had ever felt for her was gone, and she herself had
driven it away.

Gradually she stopped her frantic pacing and sat
down in the window recess to try to visualise her
future life. Maybe, if she had a child, she might find
some consolation in the dark years that lay ahead.
She stood again, but suddenly a sharp pain gripped
her—a familiar pain that told her she had been
mistaken and that Sir Ralph's hopes would come to
nothing. For a moment she felt a strange sorrow;
then, gradually, her spirits rose. There was no
reason now why she should not accompany her
husband to France. Perhaps, in some new environ-
ment, she would be able to reveal her true feelings
for him.

CHAPTER
NINE

THEY LEFT for France on a bright October day. Sails billowing in the wind sped them over the white-capped waves, and Isabel's enjoyment was so apparent that Sir Ralph looked amused.

'I see that I need have no fears for you, madam. You appear to be one of the fortunate ones who are not ill on board ship.'

Eyes sparkling, she turned to meet his admiring gaze. 'I love the movement. It does not upset me, but I fear that poor Alice is in a sad way. She is almost prostrate with sickness, and there is naught I can do for her. Now she is trying to sleep, but without much success.' She continued, 'It is the last part of our journey that makes me nervous. I am concerned that your aunt may not welcome me because I am English.'

'My aunt will love you for my sake. She is not as antagonistic towards the English as I made out to Henry. It was a small ruse I employed to stop him from insinuating himself into her household.'

She looked puzzled. 'I do not understand why you should wish to keep him away from your French relations, sir.'

'He is not to be trusted. Surely you should know that.'

She winced at the reminder. Yes, she had trusted

Henry Viner, and would have accepted his help if Anthony had been less cautious. Even now she doubted whether his offer was really as malicious as Sir Ralph had suggested. Sighing, she looked down at the tumbling waves as she heard him say,

'I think the wind will soon blow itself out. Let us hope we shall not presently be becalmed.'

'That might be very pleasant,' Isabel smiled. 'It would prolong our stay on the water, and there is no real need for haste, is there?'

She glanced up as she spoke and saw a shadow cross his face.

'I do not wish to be delayed. I have business which will entail a journey.' He hesitated for a moment. 'I shall be obliged to leave you for a few days alone with my aunt, but . . .' He caught her look of dismay. 'I assure you there will be amusement enough for you to pass the time pleasantly.'

'Business?' She stared at him blankly. 'What business can you have in France? And why must you leave me alone? May I not go with you?'

'No, madam. That, I regret, is not possible. The journey would be too hard for you.'

He had not, she noticed, answered her question fully, but there was something in his expression that deterred her from further enquiries. Disappointed and puzzled, she turned away.

'I must go below and see how Alice is faring,' she said coldly.

When, at last, they landed in Calais, the weather had deteriorated and a chill autumnal rain was falling steadily. Next morning early, under a grey sky, they set out on the last part of their journey, Isabel and Alice travelling in a hired coach—a rough uncomfortable vehicle, little more than a

wagon, which bumped and jolted so much that
Alice said it was not much better than being on the
sea.

Straining to see as much of the countryside as
possible, Isabel was disappointed to find it so dull
and uninteresting, but after two days they entered a
pretty green valley. Drawing up alongside, Sir
Ralph pointed ahead to where, high on the hillside,
a great house towered over a small village.

Half-castle, half-château, its grim forbidding ex-
terior caused Isabel to utter an exclamation of
dismay. Somehow she had imagined that Sir
Ralph's aunt would live in a cheerful, gracious
mansion, but this strange turreted building, with its
high pointed roofs and great walls, looked more of
a fortress than a family home.

'Do not look so horrified!' Sir Ralph sounded
amused as he saw her expression. 'It is very comfortable inside. My aunt does not live here all the
time. She will return to her estate in the South
before winter sets in, but while she is here I take
advantage of it to visit her.'

As they approached, the great doors opened
suddenly as though their arrival had been observed
from within. Servants appeared, the horses were
led off to the stables, and they were ushered into a
great magnificently furnished room where two
ladies waited to greet them.

Exhausted by the journey, Isabel stood suddenly
stricken by nervousness, which was increased by
her inability to understand the rapid French that
seemed quite unlike the language she had been
taught at home. Sir Ralph, however, was at his
ease, laughing and answering the questions and
exclamations of pleasure, until suddenly he

stopped, and drew Isabel forward.

She rose from a deep curtsy and, to her surprise, was immediately drawn into a warm embrace and kissed on both cheeks.

Madame de Brémont was a tall, dignified woman in her late fifties, whose face still showed traces of early beauty. Richly dressed in black velvet relieved only by a starched white ruff and two long necklaces of magnificent pearls, she stood back and surveyed Isabel with an all-enveloping glance.

'So. My new niece,' she said in English. 'How beautiful you are, *ma chère*. It is not surprising that you should have captured my nephew's heart.'

Colour flooded into Isabel's face, and she curtsied again as the other lady approached. Madame de Tanguy, explained Sir Ralph, was his aunt's cousin, and the two ladies, both widows, had lived together since the deaths of their respective husbands.

She was a small, plump woman with smiling eyes and a vivacious manner. She also spoke English, though with a strong French accent, and laughed enchantingly as she tried to make herself understood. It was plain to see that both ladies adored Sir Ralph and were prepared to give his wife equal affection. Under the influence of such a warm welcome, Isabel relaxed as she sipped wine, and felt her flagging spirits revive.

Later, when she had washed and changed her travel-stained clothes, she surveyed the vast bedchamber. A bright fire was burning in the hearth, the walls were hung with fine tapestries, and the windows looked over an enclosed garden laid out in formal fashion with box hedges and gravelled paths. At the sight of the enormous bed with its rich coverings and crimson curtains, the blood rushed to her face. Turning quickly away, she met Sir Ralph's quizzical glance.

'Do not look so nervous, my lady,' he said dryly. 'I shall sleep through there.'

He opened a door in the wall and she saw a smaller bed, another fire and a second door leading out into the corridor. She bit her lip. His mocking tone chilled her. She wanted to tell him that he was mistaken and that, in reality, she longed to give herself to him in that great bed, but it was too late. It seemed that he had lost all desire for her.

After a fine supper which went on interminably and during which she sampled many strange and exotic French dishes, they all withdrew to a smaller, less formal, room where Madame de Brémont said they would be more comfortable.

'If you are not too tired, my dear Isabel,' she said, 'please play and sing to us. I know that you English are fine musicians—will you not show us a little of your skill?'

Not daring to refuse, Isabel took the beribboned lute and searched among the music-books for something familiar. The songs were all unknown to her, and she had no wish to attempt them in front of this expectant company. At last she came upon some Latin motets that she had often sung to her parents. The fact that they were church music caused Madame de Brémont to nod approvingly, but to Isabel, tired and overwrought as she was, they brought back memories of home—memories that caused her voice to break on a sob as she sang the last Amen.

Glancing involuntarily at Sir Ralph, Isabel saw his mouth twitch in cynical amusement. She flushed guiltily. He would think her a hypocrite, singing hymns in which she no longer believed.

When they went up to the great bedchamber, he paused as he opened the door to the adjoining room. 'I shall come in when Alice has finished preparing you for bed, so do not extinguish the candles.'

She stared after him, half-frightened, half-elated. Was she to be given a second chance? Filled with joy, her whole body trembling with desire, she resolved to show that she was no longer a weeping, reluctant bride.

In an endeavour to calm herself, she purposely slowed down her preparations, discussing with Alice what she should wear next day and asking her how she had enjoyed her first few hours in a French household. But the maid seemed disinclined for gossip. From time to time she glanced anxiously at the closed door from behind which Sir Ralph could be heard moving about. Finally, as she stood brushing Isabel's hair, their eyes met in the looking-glass.

'Why, Alice!' Isabel exclaimed. 'What is amiss? Your face is troubled.'

'I cannot tell you now, my lady. Sir Ralph will become impatient. Tomorrow, if you will bear with me . . .' Alice put down the hair-brush. 'In any case, it is a small thing and will probably pass.'

'No, no,' Isabel said authoritatively. 'You shall tell me now. I do not care to lie awake wondering what is wrong with you. Come, confide in me, and I shall help you if I can.'

Alice looked anxiously again at the communicating door, then said hastily, 'There is one of the servants who is too free with his attention. Unlike the others, he speaks English, and this is useful to me, but I do not want his caresses. I fear to be alone with him.'

Isabel frowned. 'That is bad. I shall speak with Sir Ralph, and he will see that this man is warned to leave you alone. What is his name?'

'Joseph—I do not know his other name; but from the moment he saw me, and all this evening . . .' She stopped. 'Perhaps it will be better tomorrow.'

'You must not trouble yourself any more,' said Isabel. 'Are you going to be safe in your room tonight?'

'Oh, yes, my lady. I have been given a room with two other maids who seem kind and virtuous, and though I cannot understand what they say, I feel sure I shall be safe with them.' She lowered her voice, 'Madam, Sir Ralph is here.'

Curtsying quickly, she left the room, and Isabel saw her husband standing in the doorway. The firelight lit up the sheen on his brocaded dressing-gown, and he looked so tall and handsome that she longed to be enfolded in his arms. Slowly she rose to her feet.

'Pray stay seated, madam,' he said calmly. 'What I have to tell you will not take long.'

She stared at him in dismay, her dream shattered. He was as cold and distant as ever. Sick with disappointment, she sank down on the tiring-stool and clasped her hands tightly in her lap.

'I have come to tell you of my journey,' he said quietly. 'I must go tomorrow and shall probably return within a week. I leave you without undue anxiety, for'—in the mirror she could see the mockery in his eyes—'I see that you are wisely doing your best to please my aunt.'

'If you mean that I sang religious songs this evening,' she said dully, 'I assure you that I did not do so in order to ingratiate myself with Madame. I had no choice. The music-books were all strange to me, and those were the only two songs I recognised.'

'I am glad to hear it, and ask your pardon for having misjudged you.' He paused. 'Good night, madam.' He bowed as he turned to go back to his room. 'I trust you will sleep well.'

Numb with humiliation, she stared at the closed door. Then, too sorrowful even to weep, she climbed up into the great bed and lay heartsick until, at last, her burning eyes closed in sleep.

She awoke early, and the terrible sadness swept over her again. Ralph scarcely knows I am here, she thought bitterly. His mind is on his journey and his mysterious destination. What business could be so urgent that it necessitated his setting out so soon after their arrival? Vaguely she recalled some talk at table yesterday—something about a problem Madame de Brémont was having on her estate down in the South of France. But it would not be possible for him to return within a week from so far away. Suddenly she shivered, chilled by a thought that seemed to turn her heart to ice. Why had it not occurred to her sooner? These frequent visits to France could have only one meaning. A woman. A mistress who lived within reach of his aunt's château, and whom he could visit regularly under pretext of devotion to his aunt. She blinked back furious tears that threatened to overwhelm her, and buried her face in her hands.

Later, when they gathered to wish him God-speed, Isabel drew her husband aside.

'I do not remember, sir—I was tired last night, but I do not recall that you told me where you were going today.'

He looked at her seriously. 'There are friends I must visit. They will be travelling to England shortly, and I have promised to help them with their arrangements.'

She stared at him disbelievingly. 'Friends? Well, may I not accompany you? I should like to see more of this country.'

'No, madam. You must not press me. I told you before that the journey would be too rough for you. In the summer, on our next visit, I shall take you further into France.'

Her fears confirmed, Isabel said no more, and accompanied by only his body-servant and a groom, Sir Ralph rode away.

As they waved goodbye, Madame de Brémont said softly, 'Let us hope that all goes smoothly for him.'

Isabel stared. 'Why do you say that, madame? He is only going to visit friends. At least,' she added bitterly, 'that is what he told me.'

'But—but . . .' Madame de Brémont sounded startled. 'Surely you know . . .' She stopped abruptly, biting her lips, then hastily she added, 'Yes, of course, he goes to friends. But journeys in this country are always dangerous. There are many vagrants—robbers . . .' She took Isabel's arm, and as they went back indoors she said lightly, 'To help you pass the time agreeably, I suggest you come with me to call on friends of mine who live not far from here and would be delighted to meet you.'

It was, Isabel had to admit, a pleasant enough excursion. Madame de Tanguy, who was suffering from a slight fever, did not accompany them, but when at last, tired after the effort of speaking French all day, Isabel followed her hostess back into the house, they found Madame de Tanguy in a state of great excitement.

'I have had a visitor from England,' she announced. 'A most charming young man. A Monsieur Viner—a cousin of our dear Sir Ralph. He was, he said, on a short visit to France and had missed his direction. Knowing that his cousin had relations in this part of the country, he had made enquiries and decided to call on us. He could not stay long, as he wished to get to his destination before nightfall. I told him that Sir Ralph would be desolated to have missed him, and he asked where he had gone.' She hesitated, and glanced rather nervously at Madame de Brémont. 'I saw no harm in telling him that Sir Ralph was travelling southwards in the direction of Rheims to visit friends and, strangely enough, it appeared that Monsieur Viner himself was going in that direction, though he doubted if they would meet.'

'*Mon Dieu!*' Madame de Brémont exclaimed. 'Marie—you should not have told him that. Did you not remember that our nephew made us promise we would never, under any circumstances, betray his whereabouts.'

Madame de Tanguy's mouth trembled. 'But he is Sir Ralph's cousin,' she protested, 'and, as he told me, a good Catholic.' She paused. 'That is true, is it not, Isabel?'

She nodded indifferently. 'Oh, yes. He is certainly a Catholic, though Sir Ralph says he is too political for his liking.'

For a moment she wondered whether she should add that Sir Ralph did not trust his cousin, but it would no doubt distress Madame de Brémont and agitate Madame de Tanguy. Besides, why should she trouble herself about a husband who was bent only on concealing the fact that he was visiting a mistress? It was humiliating enough that she should be deceived and treated like a foolish child by these two ladies, who knew so much more than she did. She looked at them coldly.

'I must confess, mesdames, that I do not understand this secrecy. Why should there be any cause for disquiet? What is this business which takes my husband away almost as soon as we arrive?'

The two ladies glanced at each other in open consternation, and then Madame de Brémont said quietly, '*Ma chère*, we are bound by a vow of secrecy. It is painful for us to have to refuse to explain, but until Sir Ralph himself tells you, we must keep silent.'

Furiously Isabel opened her mouth to speak, then abruptly she changed her mind. It was no use. They were protecting their nephew, bound by a promise wrung out of them on some pretext or other. Probably he had told them that this was a farewell visit, and that he was about to end the relationship of which they could not approve. Pleading a headache, she retired to her room, leaving the two ladies flushed and embarrassed.

Pacing up and down, she tried to control her anger. How dare he treat her like this? But then he had told her he would seek his pleasure elsewhere, so she should have expected it. Was he going to end the liaison, or would he, each time they came to France, seek out his mistress and enjoy a week or so of her company?

Miserable and wretched, she hardly noticed that Alice had entered the room and was quietly smoothing and folding her dresses. But, at the sound of subdued sobbing, she turned quickly.

'Alice—dear Alice! What is wrong?'

'Oh, my lady!' The tears poured down Alice's face. 'I do not know which way to turn. Joseph Durand follows me everywhere, asking questions and behaving so lewdly that I am terrified.'

Guiltily Isabel remembered her promise.

'I am sorry. I have not yet had the opportunity to speak to Sir Ralph—at least, I must admit I forgot—we had other things to discuss. But now I will tell Madame de Brémont as soon as I see her.' She paused. 'What questions does he ask?'

'Strange ones.' Alice began to dry her eyes. 'He asks about Sir Ralph—what does he do in England, how does he hear Mass when it is forbidden, does he entertain priests in his house . . .'

Isabel frowned. 'This must be stopped at once. I shall go down now and tell Madame de Brémont.'

Reluctantly she went in search of her hostess, and found the two ladies talking together in Madame de Brémont's withdrawing room. No doubt, she thought bitterly, they were discussing the relative merits of Sir Ralph's wife and his mistress. Hurt pride made her resolve to show them that she did not care enough for her husband to let his behaviour disturb her.

She told them calmly of the way in which their servant was causing embarrassment to her maid, and saw the ladies' eyes widen in horror.

'Joseph Durand?' Madame de Brémont exclaimed. 'He must be the new man—I believe he was taken on to replace an old servant who died in the summer. I shall see that he is instantly dismissed. Such behaviour cannot be tolerated in my household.'

It took nearly an hour and many enquiries, however, before it was discovered that Joseph Durand had disappeared. He had taken his few belongings and walked out with no explanation.

Madame de Brémont seemed unduly perturbed, especially after Isabel informed her coldly that Joseph had seemed interested in Sir Ralph's activities, and Madame de Tanguy asked agitatedly whether perchance he was a spy.

Astonished, Isabel said scornfully, 'A spy? Here in this Catholic country? If it were in Protestant England one would expect such things, but what could he do here? Unless, of course, he is a Huguenot. These unfortunate people are persecuted in France, are they not?'

The two ladies stared at her in horror but said nothing and, content with having shot her barb, Isabel retired once more to her room. Let them see, she thought, that I am not blinded by devotion to religion. If they realise that I can think for myself, perhaps they will come to see that I am not the weak and gullible wife they suppose. That I know full well that my husband is unfaithful to me and that they are shielding and condoning his wrongdoing.

Gradually her anger subsided, but the bitterness remained. This, however, she resolved to keep hidden. Perhaps, after all, the two elderly ladies were not so much to blame. They had no control over their nephew, and it was obvious that, at first, Madame de Brémont had thought Sir Ralph had confessed his past to his wife. What was it she had said? Ah, yes—'*Surely you know*'—then she had hastily tried to cover up her indiscretion. And later she had said something about Sir Ralph telling her himself. Would he ever do that? Perhaps, when the liaison came to an end, but then there would be others—he had promised her that himself. But it was not the fault of the two ladies who, in spite of his faults, so obviously adored him, so she would not mention his absence again.

The week passed slowly. Accompanied by grooms, she went riding with Madame de Brémont to see the surrounding countryside and visited neighbours. She played and sang in the evenings, and gradually mastered a great deal of their music. They seemed on the whole to lead a secluded life in this great château, with no real entertaining apart from the occasional call from friends, but Madame de Brémont explained this by saying that their social life took place on her estate in the South of France, to which they would soon be returning.

The day of Sir Ralph's expected return was cold and wet. Supper was eaten at the usual time, which surprised Isabel, who thought it might have been held back until Sir Ralph arrived. Eventually, late in the evening, Madame de Brémont said calmly,

'I do not think he will come tonight. Travelling will be difficult in this weather. We may as well go to our beds.'

It seemed odd, somehow, Isabel thought. Almost as though Sir Ralph were not expected after all. She lay awake, wondering uneasily whether once more she had been deceived. The wind roaring down the chimney increased her melancholy, and the rain beating against the windows filled her with a sense of foreboding. At last, pulling the coverlets round her, she forced herself into a restless sleep.

She woke a few hours later, and lay wondering what it was that had disturbed her. The wind had dropped, but the rain was still falling heavily, coming down the chimney and causing the dying fire to hiss and spit. Suddenly she sat upright, listening intently. There was noise outside— horses' hooves on the gravel and—yes—surely she could hear voices? She jumped out of bed and pulled on her fur-lined dressing-gown before opening the door to peer out into the passage.

A faint glint of candlelight led her forward until, at the top of the staircase, she stopped and looked down into the great hall. A man was standing by the fire, his hands extended to the flames. For a moment she remained motionless then, as he turned, she saw that it was indeed her husband. Still she hesitated, then suddenly caught her breath as a side door opened and Madame de Brémont appeared. She was holding what looked like a cloak, and, stupefied, Isabel put her hand to her mouth as a tall woman emerged from the shadows to take it from her. Sir Ralph nodded as though in approval, and another cloaked and hooded figure—a maid-servant evidently—helped her mistress to adjust the garment round her shoulders.

Sir Ralph nodded again, and said quietly, 'You will think up some excuse for me, *ma tante*? It is dangerous to stay longer. We have been delayed enough already. Let us hope the ship will still be waiting at Calais.'

He bowed as he moved towards the great door, and drawing a long, sobbing breath, Isabel fled back to her room.

CHAPTER
TEN

NEXT MORNING, pale and calm, Isabel expressed her surprise that Sir Ralph had not yet returned.

Madame de Brémont glanced towards the window, indicating the rain, and shrugged helplessly.

'No doubt his friends will have insisted on his remaining with them until the weather clears. Do not trouble yourself, *ma chère*, he will most certainly return as soon as he is able.'

Madame de Tanguy, however, seemed to be less at ease, talking constantly of the difficulties of travel under such conditions, and glancing uneasily at Isabel when she thought she was unobserved. It might be possible, Isabel thought, to extract the truth from her eventually, though what good that would do she could not imagine. What more was there to learn? She had seen and heard enough to know that she was being horribly deceived—better to accept the fact that her husband was unfaithful, and preserve an icy silence when Sir Ralph finally returned.

Tired after her disturbed night, she returned to her room to rest after the midday meal and was lying on her bed with eyes closed when, once more, she heard the sound of horses' hooves on the gravelled drive. She stiffened. No, it could not possibly be Sir Ralph—The horses must belong to visitors, friends of the family. She closed her eyes again, resolving to keep to her room.

Suddenly Alice appeared, flushed and excited. 'My lady—Mr Viner is here again, and Madame hopes that you will come down to greet him.'

Isabel got up quickly, and while Alice tidied her hair and smoothed her dress, she found herself wondering if Henry Viner had any inkling of Sir Ralph's movements. In spite of her resolution to appear indifferent, she now wanted desperately to learn all she could.

A few minutes later she acknowledged Henry Viner's formal bow, and, sitting down, listened as with great charm and wit he made the two ladies laugh and sympathise with his account of a difficult journey in a foreign land.

Madame de Brémont soon suggested that her visitor should spend a few days with them before continuing on his way back to England, and glancing at him quickly she caught a triumphant glint in his eyes as he accepted her offer.

Confirmed in her resolve to find out all she could, she made up her mind to question him at the first possible opportunity. The moment came when Madame de Brémont went to make sure that her guest's bedchamber was being properly prepared, and Madame de Tanguy followed her in search of some music for their evening enterainment.

Gazing at Henry intently, Isabel wondered how to begin, but it was he who spoke first.

'You are, I think, suspicious of me, my lady,' he smiled gently. 'You cannot understand my reason for coming again to this house.'

Slightly taken aback by his directness, Isabel said, 'It has certainly aroused my curiosity, sir, though I must admit'—she lifted her head and looked at him steadily—'that I am glad to see you.'

He smiled again, evidently pleased by her welcome. 'You speak of your curiosity, but mine is infinitely greater, as your husband well knows. I have long wanted to make the acquaintance of his French relations, but he has always seemed reluctant to allow me that privilege. To a man of my enquiring nature, that has been a challenge.' He paused. 'I, for my part, am puzzled that your husband should have left you so soon after your arrival. I find such behaviour extremely odd—so beautiful a bride left alone to languish in this isolated place.'

Isabel hesitated. Something about this man repelled her, something she could not put into words. It was a feeling, uneasy and fearful, and one that seemed to tell her she must be on her guard against his outward charm. But the only one who had said he was not to be trusted was her husband, and he had shown himself to be deceitful indeed. Perhaps in Henry Viner she might find a friend to advise her. He had offered to help her once before; she would ask him to help her now.

She got up and moved restlessly about the room, and Henry watched her for a few minutes in silence. At last he said, 'My lady, I see that you are troubled. Is there something you do not understand? Will you not tell me?'

She turned abruptly and studied him closely. He looked at her kindly but still she hesitated, remembering that Anthony had also distrusted him. But he had been wrong. If he had accepted the help offered, he would not have died needlessly. All her fears undoubtedly stemmed from that time, and were probably quite unjustified.

She drew a long breath. 'Sir—I shall be frank with you. I think Sir Ralph has a mistress in this country whom he has gone to visit.'

'A mistress?' Henry stared at her incredulously. 'That is unbelievable, madam. And married such a short time! What grounds do you have for such an accusation? Why do you suspect him?'

'I—I . . .' She tried to find words, then suddenly she realised that she could not, after all, tell him everything. To do so would mean disclosing the true facts of her marriage. She could not, for very shame, confess that Sir Ralph had been to her bed for one night only, and that he had hinted he would seek his pleasure elsewhere. The colour flooded into her face, and she stayed silent while Henry stroked his beard and gazed at her thoughtfully.

At last he said softly, 'It is, of course, possible—. my cousin has always been a favourite with the Court in England and, no doubt, here in France— but, my lady,' he paused, eyebrows raised, 'I am somewhat surprised that you should be so perturbed at your husband's supposed infidelity. I had thought you to be indifferent to his charms.'

Her colour faded as she gained control of her feelings, leaving her outwardly calm.

'I think no wife, sir—however unloving—cares to be deceived.'

'However unloving . . .' he murmured, and nodded reflectively. Strolling over to the window, he stood deep in thought, then turned abruptly. 'What would you do if you discovered that your suspicions were correct? Would you retaliate by taking a lover yourself, or are you too saintly to break your marriage vows?'

Angry at the hint of mockery in his tone, she said coldly, 'I am no saint, sir. I lost my faith in God when I lost Anthony.'

'Lost your faith?' he exclaimed sharply and, taking a step forward, he put his hands on her shoulders, grasping her tightly so that she could not move away. 'Is this true? Do you no longer believe in the Church—in the Catholic cause?'

'I hold no religious cause worth while, sir.' She held still in his grasp. 'Anthony was a Protestant, yet he gave his life to save my family. I think now that one religion is as good—or as bad—as another.'

'So . . .' He released her and stood back. 'What say you to those priests who defy Queen Elizabeth in order to preach their religion?'

For a moment she hesitated as she recalled the grave and courageous young priest who had married her to Sir Ralph. 'I think,' she said at last, 'that they are brave but foolish men who risk their lives for a lost cause.'

'I am of your opinion, my lady. And what say you to those who help them to enter the country—are they not traitors?'

She shrugged, anxious now to finish this conversation, which seemed to her to be pointless. She sat down and picked up her embroidery. 'I do not know such men. How can I judge?'

Glancing up, she was surprised to see Henry go quickly to the door and peer down the passage. Apparently satisfied, he returned and stood looking down at her astonished face.

'Why so furtive, sir?' she demanded. 'There is no

need for secrecy. It seems that you cannot help me in discovering my husband's mistress, therefore we have nothing to say that may not be overheard.'

'I have much to say, but this is not the place.' His face was grim. 'I would, however, ask you one question: if you could be certain that your husband has deceived you, would you wish to be revenged on him?'

She stiffened in her chair as his meaning penetrated. So he knew more than he pretended. Suddenly she realised that, more than anything, she wanted to find out about her rival. Whether or not the knowledge would help her, she did not care, but know she must. His cold eyes were staring down at her.

'If I knew for certain who the lady was . . .' she began, and Henry said sharply, 'There is no need to hesitate, madam. I read your thoughts. You have no love for Ralph and would not be sorry to see his downfall.'

Puzzled, yet relieved at his misinterpretation, she said quietly, 'If he loves another woman, he is no husband to me.'

He seemed satisfied with that, and turned sharply as the door opened to admit Madame de Tanguy.

'I have been seeking a song that I hope Isabel will sing for us, but I cannot lay my hands on it. Perhaps it is here after all.'

She began searching among the music-books, and Henry walked across to the window.

'The rain has stopped at last.' Turning to Isabel, he added softly, 'The wind will soon dry the ground. Will you come riding with me tomorrow morning?'

He looked at her meaningfully, and Isabel nodded her assent.

Madame de Tanguy looked up. 'I have found that song. It was too difficult for me, but I am sure you could play it for us. Will you study it for a while?'

Taking the music-sheet, Isabel pretended to be absorbed, and Henry bowed courteously and left the room.

Next day the weather had improved. Dressed in a riding-habit of green velvet, Isabel saw open admiration in Henry's eyes. He himself was in more sober attire, for which he apologised.

'My journey in France has been hampered by the loss of my servant,' he said as their horses picked their way carefully down the still muddy hillside. 'He was taken ill the first night I arrived, so I was obliged to leave him in Calais. He assured me he would be recovered by the time I return. A few days ago I found another man to take his place, and he lodges down there in the village. He does not care to come to Madame de Brémont's household. He was once a servant here, he says, but was unjustly dismissed.'

Isabel turned in the saddle. 'Unjustly dismissed? Is his name Joseph Durand?'

'Why, yes. You know of him?'

She frowned. 'I never saw him, but he annoyed Alice, my maid, with his attentions. Madame de Brémont was about to dismiss him, but he could not be found. He asked so many questions that we thought he was a spy.'

'A spy? Oh, that is too much!' Henry burst out laughing. 'He is but a peasant. However, he speaks good English, which he learnt while in the service of a rich nobleman. I intend to take him back to England with me, along with the man who waits in Calais.'

They rode on in silence until Henry pointed ahead. 'Do you see that small church? I suggest we stop there and find somewhere to talk.'

Tethering the horses, they walked slowly round the outside of the building.

'Now,' Henry spoke urgently, 'I have a plan. If you will help me in this, I may be able to discover the identity of Sir Ralph's mistress. This is what I would have you do.'

Isabel listened in silence, her face gradually becoming scarlet with anger. 'I am no spying woman, sir! I will not search among my husband's papers or look through his baggage for letters to give to you. If that is what you expect of me, you are sadly mistaken.'

'But what harm is there in that?' He took her outburst calmly. 'I do not ask you to read the letters, although I have no doubt that they will appear quite innocent. But there will be secrets hidden in the words, which I will be able to decipher. Probably you will find nothing, for Sir Ralph is too clever to leave valuable information behind him. Nevertheless, you may come across something which, although meaningless to you, would enable me to trace his movements and discover the identity of the lady concerned.' He laughed unpleasantly. 'It would be interesting then to tell his aunt that the dear nephew she admires so much and to whom, as she told me herself last night, she intends to leave her estates, is not as truthful and honest as she supposes.'

Isabel stared at him in disgust, seeing him clearly

for the first time. He was not concerned for her. All he wanted to do was to harm his cousin. Furiously, without thinking, she said, 'His aunt knows full well where Sir Ralph has gone, though she will not tell me. And I myself know more than I have said. Two nights ago, Sir Ralph returned in secret. I was in bed, and heard horses, so I left my room to see what had caused the disturbance. Sir Ralph had with him a lady and her maid-servant. Madame de Brémont wished them God-speed, and they set off for Calais.' She paused, remembering her sorrow and dismay at the sight of those half-concealed figures in the shadows of the great hall. 'All I wish is to discover this lady's name. I had thought that you might help me, but I see now that you know no more than I do.'

She turned on her heel and began walking towards the horses, but Henry moved quickly and, taking her arm, swung her round to face him.

'A lady and her maid, you say. Did you speak to them?' His eyes seemed to blaze down into hers and suddenly, cruelly, he shook her violently. 'Tell me'—he repeated harshly—'did you speak to them?'

She was frightened now. His face was contorted and his fingers dug into her arm. Gasping with terror she cried out, and abruptly his manner changed. Loosening his hold on her, he forced a wintry smile.

'I regret treating you so roughly, my lady, but the fact that you had not been frank with me angered me unduly. Come, let us sit here awhile.' He led her to a stone bench against the west wall, and uneasily she sat down. 'Now tell me how you saw this mysterious lady and her maid, and what was said between you.'

Isabel drew a long breath to calm herself. Somehow she must get away from this sinister man, but in order to do so she realised that she must placate him.

'I was hidden and watching from above. They were on the point of departure. I heard Sir Ralph say that he prayed the ship would still be waiting at Calais. Then, angry at his deceit, I went back to my room. I said nothing the next day, for I knew that no one would tell me. Now, sir,' she looked at him appealingly, 'please let us go back. I see that there is nothing you can do to help me.'

He stared at her in silence, searching her face as though to make sure she had told all she knew. At last he said, 'Very well. But rest assured that I shall find out the identity of this mysterious lady and her companion.'

'No.' Isabel shook her head and looked away. 'I have changed my mind. I do not wish to pry any further. I am sure now that my husband is unfaithful, but I must learn to accept it.'

She rose from the bench and began to walk away, but suddenly he pulled her back and forced her to look at him. 'You cannot spend your life without love,' he said thickly. 'Ralph is worthless and a cold husband, but I shall be your lover. Come to me, and together we shall rid ourselves of him.'

Shocked and terrified, she gazed at him. Henry's open hatred of his cousin seemed almost abnormal. In spite of her longing to escape from him, intuition told her that she must question him and try to discover what was in his mind. 'Rid me of my husband? And how would you do that, sir?'

'Ah!' he smiled delightedly. 'So you are interested. Well, I shall tell you. There are several ways in which he could be destroyed and deprived of his possessions. There are accusations which, with a little more proof, I could make against him. There is the fact that you, his wife, do not love him and could possibly be persuaded to discover and divulge secret activities, in which I am convinced he is heavily involved.' He stopped, as Isabel stared at him in disgust.

'That is your great desire, then?' Her voice trembled. 'You covet his wealth and would stop at nothing to step into his shoes?'

'You would be the one to step into them, madam,' he smiled grimly. 'But with my shoes along with yours under the same bed, we would have a very pleasant life. Since you no longer believe in the Catholic Church and I have a great dislike of paying fines, we could live freely as ornaments of the Protestant Church of which the Queen is head and thus enjoy great favour and privilege.'

She frowned. 'And what of the Queen of Scots? I thought you desired to see her on the throne of England. You were ardent enough in her cause when you were in my father's house.'

He bowed mockingly, sure now of her connivance, as she meant him to be. 'My lady, that I have often expressed such opinions I freely admit, but I do so only in order to learn who is for and who is against a revolution—for that is what it would mean. I would not endanger my life for either queen. If ever Mary Stuart should triumph, I would be her most devoted Catholic servant. I am willing to bend my conscience either way—it is only thus that one can hope to advance in the world.'

She nodded thoughtfully as though appreciating his point of view, but a wave of nausea swept over her at the realisation of his unscrupulous self-seeking. At last she said, 'I have a bad headache, sir. I should like to go back now. Will you help me to mount?'

For a moment he hesitated; then, with a quick glance at her pale face, he took her arm and led her towards the waiting horses.

The two ladies were full of concern at her pretended indisposition, and she yielded easily to their suggestion that she should go to bed. After submitting to their anxious ministrations, she expressed a great desire for sleep, and eventually they left her in peace. Alone at last, she tried to assemble her thoughts.

Why had Henry become so violent when he demanded to know if she had spoken to the mysterious women she had glimpsed the other night? What did he mean when he spoke of possible accusations for which he needed more proof? And what was this talk of secret activities in which he said Sir Ralph was involved?

The last question lingered in her mind. There was something familiar about the suggestion that he might be engaged in secret work. Someone had once said—Ah! Her pulses began to race as a scene from the past flashed with startling clarity in front of her eyes. Her father, recently back from the Tower, praising Sir Ralph—'*A staunch Catholic. He does much work for our hunted priests*'. When she had mentioned it to Sir Ralph, he had seemed angry and said that her father was indiscreet and told her not to repeat the tale. But, later, he himself had spoken of seminary priests travelling from one Catholic house to another. They needed help, he had told her, horses, clothes, disguises—disguises! She sat bolt upright in bed, staring unseeingly ahead as everything fell into place at last.

That tall lady she had foolishly supposed to be her husband's mistress—the maid-servant—priests from Rheims seminary. Why yes, Madame de Tanguy had said that that was the direction in which Sir Ralph had gone! Here, in this isolated château they obtained the clothes necessary to conceal their identity before they were escorted to Calais and met by friends on their arrival at Dover. Oh, God! What dangerous work! She shuddered violently at the thought of the penalties Sir Ralph and his associates risked. Imprisonment, torture—a fearful death on the scaffold. No wonder the utmost secrecy had to be observed. One careless remark, and all could be lost, for spies were always listening.

Spies! Again an icy hand seemed to grip her heart. Henry Viner must be a spy. It was apparent from his questions. He had guessed at once that the supposed mistress and her maid were priests. That was why he became so violent, knowing that he had missed his chance of following them. So now he would stay here, ferreting out all the information he could in order to report to his master, Sir Francis Walsingham, the Queen's Secretary of State and head of the Secret Service, whose spies and agents were to be found everywhere. Sir Ralph had warned her to be discreet for her own good, but why, oh why, had he not told her of his dangerous work? His aunt and her cousin knew, indeed they were as deeply involved as he was, but he had kept his wife in ignorance of the perilous life he led. Perhaps he wished to spare her the anxiety she would feel—No, of course that was not the reason. It was because he did not wholly trust her in view of her attitude towards the Church. It was her own fault, and now he was in grave danger as a direct result of her own jealousy of a woman who did not exist.

Jumping out of bed, she tried to control her trembling hands as she dressed. She must be ready so that as soon as Sir Ralph returned she could warn him. She must also tell Madame de Brémont and her cousin that she had discovered their secret, and put them on their guard. Madame de Tanguy in particular must be warned, as she had already said too much to Henry Viner.

They were delighted to see that she had made such a quick recovery, and she was just about to confide in them when, to her dismay, Henry came into the room.

He greeted her smilingly and, after a few moments' polite conversation, suggested a walk in the Long Gallery, ostensibly to give her opinion on one of the portraits hanging there.

As soon as they were safely out of earshot, he said urgently, 'You said, my lady, that you had no further wish to discover the identity of your husband's mistress, but I have decided to continue the search, both for your eventual happiness and for my own.' He smiled grimly. 'One day you will, I think, be glad to seek my protection.'

Anxious to learn all she could of his future plans, she contented herself with a careless shrug. 'Will you return to England, sir?'

He hesitated, and now that she knew every word he uttered was a lie, she watched him carefully.

'Soon, I think. To London first, then down to Dorset.' He paused. 'How long do you suppose your visit here will last?'

'I know nothing of my husband's plans'—she managed to inject a note of bitterness into her voice. 'His aunt will no doubt wish him to stay for a while longer, as she has not yet had much opportunity of enjoying his company.'

'That is true.' He eyed her narrowly. 'Once his mistress is safely installed in England, he can afford to dally here in France. You will, I gather, have company with you on your return journey. Madame de Tanguy has told me that there are friends of his living in this country who may well travel with you.'

'Friends?' Her voice faltered. Why was Madame de Tanguy so indiscreet? It was plain to see that, not having been warned, she imagined Henry to be trustworthy. She tried to speak lightly. 'Surely not another mistress, sir? That would be too much.'

He laughed harshly. 'I see that you are coming to appreciate how false a husband he is. But from what Madame de Tanguy tells me, these are friends of long standing. Men of law who are desirous of visiting our universities.'

'Madame de Tanguy knows more than I do.' She shrugged once more, and made to turn away as though bored with the conversation.

'Then the sooner you learn all you can, the better for you, my lady,' he said roughly. 'That is, if you wish to achieve your desire.'

'You speak in riddles, sir,' she said calmly. 'Why should I trouble myself with my husband's affairs? I tell you truthfully, I have lost interest in his sordid intrigues.'

He said nothing for a few moments, but she saw his mouth tighten. Then, taking her arm, he led her down the gallery, until he turned to face her by the west window. 'There is more to this business than you suppose. Sir Ralph is involved in activities that are frowned on in England.'

Isabel's heart began to race. Was he now going to tell her what she had already discovered? Purposely misunderstanding him, she stared at him in dismay.

'What can you mean, sir? Are you hinting that, in spite of all he has said, Sir Ralph is plotting for the Queen of Scots? He who professes such loyalty to Queen Elizabeth? I find that hard to believe.'

He hesitated, and she saw in his eyes that she had provided him with a way in which he could arouse her indignation. He could not be sure that she would collaborate with him if he spoke of seminary priests, for she had told him she thought they were brave if foolish, and she probably would not sympathise with him in his wish to betray them. He could not afford to risk her becoming so angry that she would warn her husband.

'Sir Ralph is involved in treachery,' he said at last. 'But you, my lady, I know are loyal to Her Grace. If I had more proof, I could move against him, but I must know his future plans. If you wish to be rid of him, you have only to listen and pass all information on to me. These friends of his are, without doubt, traitors—working for France and the Queen of Scots and bent on destroying the peace of our country. I would like to know the day they arrive here, and when you all plan to leave for Calais. Then I would see to it that they are arrested as soon as they land at Dover.'

'You are right, sir. I hate lies and treachery, and am most certainly not for the Queen of Scots. If Sir Ralph is involved in such horrible schemes, then I—I . . .' She sank down on the window-seat and looked up at Henry in well-simulated indignation. 'How can I pass on information to you? Will you remain here to confront Sir Ralph?'

He laughed grimly, triumphant at her apparent anger. 'No, no. That would be too soon. I leave here tomorrow, but I shall not be far away. Joseph Durand is in the village, and will come to me immediately he receives a message from you.'

Another spy! With horror she realised the enormous net in which she was caught, a net spun in England by that monster Walsingham, which would eventually emmesh Ralph and his friends like helpless flies.

'You understand, do you not?' Henry spoke impatiently. 'I wish to catch the traitors who travel in your party. You yourself will come to no harm, but Ralph will be unmasked and will suffer his just deserts.' His tone changed, 'Then, my sweet lady, you and I shall reap the reward, for I have been promised that, although a traitor's estates usually revert to the Crown, in this case, in view of my loyalty, they will be given to me.'

He took her hand and pulled her up. 'You know that I am your friend, do you not? I offered to help you once before, and I think you trusted me then. Will you not trust me now?'

Hating him, loathing his proximity, she managed to give him a calculating look. 'You say that

Ralph's estates have been promised to you, sir.
What, then, of me? You told me I would inherit his
possessions.'

He bit his lip. He had said too much. But,
recovering himself quickly, he said smoothly, 'That
was before your marriage, my lady. I have been
engaged in Sir Francis Walsingham's service for
many months, and your wedding, if you remember,
was so secret that no one is aware that you are now
Sir Ralph's heir. Naturally, in view of your inno-
cence, you would be allowed ample provision.' He
paused. 'But one thing more. Now that you understand the situation, I must ask you again to search
your husband's baggage. It is a thing that only you
can do. Do it this evening, for I leave tomorrow.'
His eyes narrowed. 'Perhaps it would be better if I
came to your room myself when everyone is in bed.
Then we could search together.'

'Oh, no!' Her heart thudding fiercely sent the
blood rushing to her face, and thankfully she realised that it looked as though she feared for her
virtue. 'That is far too dangerous. I shall search
well. You may trust me.'

He laughed. 'So you would keep me at arm's
length yet awhile. But it shall be as you wish.' He
swept her a bow. 'Now I must go to talk with Joseph
Durand.'

Alone at last, she sank once more on to the
window-seat, trembling still at the ordeal she had
undergone. If only Sir Ralph would return! Surely,
if he were only going to Calais, he should come
soon? How could she bear the burden of her terrible discovery alone? Was there no one to whom
she could turn for help? Ah, but there was!
Madame de Brémont and Madame de Tanguy must

be warned at once, and then perhaps they could think of some scheme whereby Sir Ralph and his friends could be saved.

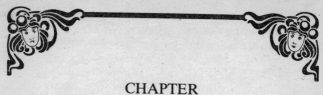

CHAPTER
ELEVEN

WHITE-FACED, the two ladies sat listening to Isabel and, by the time she came to the end of her story, tears were welling up in Madame de Tanguy's eyes. Madame de Brémont glanced at her quickly, then patted her on the shoulder.

'We are both to blame,' she said. 'You, admittedly, were indiscreet, but I trusted Monsieur Viner too, and invited him to stay with us. However, there is naught to be gained by reproaching ourselves. We must think hard and discuss what we can do to outwit this evil man.'

She reached forward and clasped Isabel's hands in hers. 'From what you have told us, my very dear niece, I can see that you have acted most courageously. As you have guessed, Sir Ralph is engaged in dangerous work, and now I shall tell you how it is done. In England there is a wealthy Catholic—Gilbert White—who has gathered together a group of about thirty young men who are bound by a vow to help the Church in her hour of need. They call themselves the League of Young Gentlemen, and Sir Ralph is one of their most daring members. They meet the priests from France, supply them with money and the necessities of life and put them in touch with Catholic families. Your husband's frequent visits to France are explained by his devotion to me, his aunt, and in truth *ma chère*, we—Marie and I—are proud to help these brave young men in our own small way.'

Her cousin nodded in agreement. 'We were astonished at first that he had told you nothing, but then we decided that it must have been because he did not wish you to suffer any fears on his behalf.'

Madame de Brémont said impatiently, 'Yes, yes. But we must not waste time in idle talk.' She looked at Isabel. 'You say that Monsieur Viner is planning to leave here tomorrow—we must see that he does, for we expect more priests from Rheims to arrive this evening to stay with us until Sir Ralph returns from Calais.'

'*Mon Dieu!*' Suddenly Madame de Tanguy burst into a paroxysm of grief. 'I told him—I told Monsieur Viner that Ralph would be travelling to England with some friends.'

'Marie!' Madame de Brémont stared at her cousin in horror. 'Did you—No, surely you could not have said they were priests from Rheims?'

'*Mais non, mais non!*' Madame de Tanguy said indignantly. 'They were men of law, I said, wishing to visit the English universities. That is how Ralph told us they would be travelling.'

Isabel nodded. 'Henry Viner told me that that was what you had said, but he does not believe it. He said they were traitors working for the Queen of Scots. He will not admit to me that he is a priest-hunter.'

Madame de Tanguy wrung her hands. 'What must we do? What can we do?'

Madame de Brémont drew a long breath and sat in silence for a minute. Then she said, 'We must act as though nothing unusual is afoot. We are expecting guests. What is strange about that? One thing we have learnt which is greatly to our advantage is that there are spies all around us. Monsieur Viner—for he will not go far away—Joseph Durand, and possibly others of whose existence we are not aware. So'—she glanced quickly at Madame de Tanguy—'we must not confide in anyone, however trustworthy they may appear. If Ralph returns safely, then . . .'

'If?' Isabel exclaimed in alarm. 'Why do you say "if", Madame?'

'There is always doubt, *ma petite*,' Madame de Brémont said gently. 'I do not think Ralph intended to cross over to England with the two priests dressed as women—arrangements were made to meet them at Dover—but if because of the heavy gales they had to take a different ship, he might have decided to travel with them in case they should miss the young men who were to escort them inland. It is the arrival in England that is so dangerous. If an informer has been at work, as soon as they set foot on English soil . . .' She stopped as she saw the horror in Isabel's eyes, and went on slowly. 'If he returns safely this time, I think we must try to persuade him to give up this work. He is married now, and I think it is wrong to endanger his life in this way. That is my view, and I shall not hesitate to put it to him.'

That evening, as they sat at table, Henry Viner was at his most charming, and Madame de Brémont and her cousin, successfully hiding their true feelings, responded laughingly to his witticisms. The time passed pleasantly with no sign of strain but, before retiring for the night, Henry drew Isabel aside.

'I shall leave tomorrow morning,' he said softly. 'I hope you will have made the necessary search by then. Do not forget—all papers, letters, small books—anything you think might interest me.'

'Yes, yes, I understand, sir. But . . .' She shrugged. 'Why you should imagine that Sir Ralph would be so foolish as to leave behind him any papers that could be made to appear incriminating, I cannot imagine. None the less,' she paused, seeing that he did not care for her vague defence of her husband, 'I shall do as you wish, and before you leave tomorrow I hope to have something for you that will assist in your work. I think'—she looked at him steadily—'that it is a noble task, for you are doing your best to unmask those who plot against the Queen's Grace.'

He glanced quickly towards the other end of the room, where Madame de Brémont and Madame de Tanguy were engaged in low-voiced conversation.

'You must not talk so clearly. If those ladies should suspect you, they would not hesitate to denounce you to your husband. Remember, they are French, and as such have every desire to see the Queen of Scots—their former Queen—on the throne of England.'

Later Isabel sat in her bedchamber deep in thought, while Alice prepared her for sleep. She had no intention of searching Sir Ralph's belongings, but somehow she would have to make Henry believe she had done as he wished. Drawing her breath in a long sigh, she saw Alice looking at her doubtfully.

'Madam . . .' The girl's voice trembled. 'Today I saw Joseph Durand. He came to the house asking if he could work here again. The Steward sent him away, but before he left he drew me aside. The things he told me made me tremble for Sir Ralph's safety.'

Isabel whirled round to face her. 'What did he say? What do you know?'

Alice bit her lip nervously. 'Do not be angry with me, my lady. I only wish to help you. That is why I listened to him, pretending that I liked him in order to learn his secrets.'

Even in her agitation, Isabel could not help an involuntary smile. 'Dear Alice, how can I scold you when you have played the same game as I have? Indeed, I would laugh if I were not so troubled, for you and I are women together and use the same weapons.'

The girl stared at her in bewilderment. 'I do not understand! You . . .'

'Never mind that now. I will explain later, for I see that you must be told everything in order to help us. What did Joseph say?'

'I could scarcely believe it—Sir Ralph . . . Madam, is it true that he helps traitors to enter England to cause great trouble, even war between England and Scotland?' She frowned. 'I do not understand these great affairs, but Joseph said it was to do with politics, and that Sir Ralph was a traitor to his country.' She drew a long, shuddering breath. 'He told me that if I wanted to help the Catholic cause in England I must pass on information to him. That way, he said, I would be working for the Church, because men like Sir Ralph were doing harm to the Catholic cause by bringing in traitors to make war in the country.' She wrung her hands, her pretty face white with fear. 'Madam, tell me it is not true! That Sir Ralph is no traitor.'

'Sit down, Alice.' Isabel pointed to a stool. 'Listen carefully, and I shall tell you how you have been tricked.'

The fire had died down and the candles were burning low in their sockets by the time she finished. It had been difficult to explain, but it was, she perceived, going to be even harder to impress on Alice that she must hide her agitation and, if necessary, act as go-between, and pass on false information through Joseph Durand in order to deceive Henry Viner. For even while she had been unfolding her story, Isabel had begun to see how she could help Sir Ralph. Joseph Durand's intentions were plain enough. He meant Alice to tell her mistress, and thereby show her the way in which reports could be passed on to his master. Obviously he was acting on Henry Viner's instructions. Well, two could play at that game, and she might be able to mislead him enough to save Sir Ralph from falling into his trap.

As simply as she could, she explained her plan, and when she saw that Alice had fully understood, she added, 'You were courageous enough to help Anthony and me, and now I am asking you to join me in a much greater undertaking. I shall not, however, force you to do anything against your will. You are free to choose and, if you do not wish to take part in this dangerous work, I will try to find another way.'

Alice sat for a few moments in silence. 'How can I refuse, my lady?' she said simply. 'It is not much that you ask me to do. I will help you gladly.'

Next morning Henry Viner made his farewells and thanked Madame de Brémont for her hospitality. Turning to Isabel, he said courteously, 'If you have any messages you would like me to pass on, either to your servants at Overton Place or to your parents, whose house will be on my route to the West Country, I shall gladly do so.'

Isabel hesitated and then, as Madame de Brémont withdrew discreetly, he added quickly, 'Well, did you find aught of interest to me?'

'There is nothing there. I saw no papers, nothing that could possibly assist you, sir. I was disappointed, for I had hoped . . .' She shrugged despondently. 'Sir Ralph has left nothing to chance.'

'I am astonished!' Henry's voice was rough with anger. 'I should have thought you would have found some small indication of his future plans—some figures jotted down to indicate dates of travel. Are you certain that you searched thoroughly?'

She stared at him indignantly. 'I am no fool, sir. I am as dismayed as you. When he returns, I shall search again as soon as I can find an opportunity. It is possible that he may have papers then that I can copy out for you.'

He nodded, and then, as he bowed and made to leave her, she added,

'My maid, who now has a liking for Joseph Durand, has agreed to pass on messages to you. I have explained all to her, and she is anxious to help.'

His cold eyes glinted and she saw that he was pleased. Bending down, he kissed her hand, and she steeled herself to let her fingers linger in his.

'I look forward to our next meeting, madam,' he said softly.

She watched him ride away and then went in

search of Madame de Brémont and her cousin to tell them what she had planned.

'Let us hope Sir Ralph returns soon,' said Madame de Tanguy. She looked searchingly at Isabel. 'You are so pale, my dear; we must bring back the colour to your cheeks. Would you like to come with me to visit our neighbours? It will take your mind off your troubles.'

Madame de Brémont agreed. 'Yes, do that, *ma chère*. I must stay here to make sure all things are prepared for our guests, who will, I trust, arrive this evening.'

It was a crisp, bright day and the bracing air helped to clear some of the anxiety from Isabel's mind, but she was thankful when at last they returned to the château. The air was colder now, with a hint of frost, and there were great fires glowing in the rooms as they entered.

Madame de Brémont greeted them joyfully. 'A messenger has come with good news. Ralph is on his way. He will arrive tonight. Our guests are already here. They are changing their clothes, and we shall all meet in the gallery before supper.'

Alice was waiting in the bedchamber, and as she helped Isabel out of her riding-habit, she spoke of the new arrivals. 'I saw them come, my lady. Young men, all three dressed plainly. Indeed they look what they pretend to be, sober and serious men of law. It is hard not to treat them with extra reverence.'

'You must not think of them in that way,' Isabel said firmly, 'or you will betray them to spying eyes.' She added briskly, 'Now, what shall I wear in honour of these legal gentlemen?'

The Long Gallery was ablaze with candles when

she entered, and the three gentlemen rose at her approach, and bowed. Madame de Brémont made the presentations and soon, as she drank her wine, Isabel was able to study the new arrivals.

The oldest one, a man she judged to be in his mid-thirties and who went by the name of Jean Roget, was tall and black-bearded with a ready smile. He seemed to be the leader of the trio. Pierre Duval was a small wiry-looking man with an ascetic face, and his companion, Bernard le Brun with his brown hair and sallow complexion, lived up to his name. He would have seemed inconspicuous but for his keen dark eyes which glinted with humour at his friends' light-hearted conversation.

Later, seated at table, they spoke of Edmund Campion and two other priests who had been captured at the same time. They were well informed of the latest developments and seemed to have no illusions as to their probable fate. Isabel marvelled as they spoke calmly of the horrors of Tyburn and, seeing their eyes glow in the candlelight, she realised that each priest had already accepted a similar destiny. Such cool courage filled her with awe and a sudden understanding of the motive that made men like Sir Ralph undertake to help them in their perilous task.

The evening wore on and still Sir Ralph did not return. Sick with anxiety, Isabel went at last to her bedchamber and, after dismissing Alice, sat in her dressing-gown by the fire, her thoughts reaching out to her husband. Was he, she wondered, thinking of her as he rode through the cold night, or was he so absorbed in his plans to help the new arrivals that there was no room in his heart for her? She shivered involuntarily as a picture formed in her memory. Once before, a young man had ridden through the dark in order to save others from peril. She had thought her heart would break when they told her how Anthony had died, and yet here she sat, her heart full to overflowing with love for another man. How, she wondered, could she have changed so much in the course of a few months?

A log fell to the hearth, sending sparks flying up the chimney, and as she bent to mend the fire, she saw how the flames burnt even more brightly as a fresh log fed on the red-hot embers. So, she reflected, had her heart been mended, the old love having laid the foundation for a greater, stronger, more lasting one. The fire in her heart was burning now as it had never burned for her kind and gentle Anthony. Perhaps, she thought sadly, she had loved him only because he loved her, responding to him with a girl's instinctive wish to be cherished and adored. What was it Sir Ralph had said that time in the garden of her old home? 'A childish friendship'—That was hard, but there was truth in it. There was nothing childish in this new phoenix-like flame that enveloped her whole being as she waited for his return.

She got up and moved restlessly about the room, then suddenly, with a great leap of her heart, she heard the sound for which she had been longing. Horses' hooves, the jingling of harness, voices and the noise of doors being flung open. Sitting down again, she tried to control her shaking limbs. How hard it was to wait and listen for the door in the corridor to open. Would he come into her room, or would he suppose her to be sleeping in calm in-difference to his return?

He must have opened the door very quietly, for

suddenly he was there, standing behind her, and for a moment she thought she would faint as she turned and saw him.

He took a step forward, his arms outstretched. 'Madam, what is wrong? Are you ill?'

Longing to throw herself into his embrace, she stared at him, and slowly he dropped his arms and remained still, his eyes fixed on her with an unreadable expression in their dark depths.

Her throat dry, she swallowed hard and said huskily, 'I must talk with you. It is a long story.'

He bowed, pulled up a chair and, gazing at her with raised eyebrows, waited until she felt able to begin.

The fire was sinking by the time her tale was done, and all the while he sat in silence gazing at her with that strange expression on his face. At last she sank back exhausted and closed her eyes, unable to bear his searching look any longer. When she opened them again, he was on his feet, regarding her closely.

'You have engaged yourself in a dangerous game, madam. Why have you done so much for me?'

She saw that his face was pale and drawn. 'Did you expect me to do nothing? To let you fall into a trap that would lead to the death of those brave priests, and very probably your own as well?'

'I should have thought it would have suited you to be rid of me, madam. You would have gained much, and lost your hated husband.'

His voice was so harsh that she clasped her hands together convulsively and looked away.

Now was her chance to tell him of her love, but under his stern scrutiny, she found herself speechless. It was no use, she told herself desperately. She could not risk the humiliation of being rejected. She swallowed, trying to loosen the constriction in her throat. 'Just as you are loyal to the Queen, sir, and do not wish for her downfall, so am I loyal to my husband.'

She saw a muscle twitch in his face, and then he said, 'For that I thank you, madam, I am greatly in your debt. Tomorrow we shall decide what we must do in order to outwit Walsingham and his spies.' He placed his hand gently on her shoulder. 'You may be sure we shall find a way, so let your sleep be easy.' He bowed deeply, and hesitated for a moment. 'Good night, madam.'

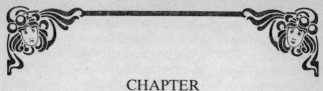

CHAPTER
TWELVE

NEXT MORNING Sir Ralph had his plans ready and, in a quiet parlour, he told the assembled company of Isabel's discovery. Then he added, 'I had thought to accompany my guests to Calais in a week's time and see them on board ship, knowing that they would be met by friends at Dover. This must now be changed. Delay, I think, will increase the danger. So this is what I propose. My wife's maid will go to Joseph Durand and tell him that we shall be leaving here for Calais in five days' time. Certainly, in five days, a party of servants with baggage will set off, but neither I nor you three gentlemen will be with them. We shall leave here tomorrow night in the utmost secrecy and make for Boulogne. I shall accompany you to England, for when we arrive at Rye, we shall not be met as there is no time to make the necessary arrangements. I shall then take you to friends who will help you to set out on your journeys.'

The priests agreed, as calmly, thought Isabel, as though they were setting out on a hawking-party. Suddenly she looked up.

'May I not travel with you, Sir Ralph? Nay, do not shake your head so vigorously, I pray you, sir. Surely it would allay suspicion, for no one would expect seminary priests to be in the company of a lady and her maid.'

None of them replied immediately. The priests glanced at each other quizzically, and Sir Ralph's brows drew together in a deep frown. At last Madame de Brémont commented. 'I think your wife's request is reasonable, sir. My cousin and I shall be sad to lose her, but in truth it would be strange indeed if you left her behind while you escorted guests to England.'

Sir Ralph's frown deepened. 'I cannot like it. The danger . . .' He turned to Isabel. 'It would be a long, hard journey for you and your woman. No coach—for we must travel swiftly.' He got up and moved restlessly about the room, passing his hand across his forehead. Suddenly he wheeled round. 'No! She must remain here till I return to fetch her.'

'Ah, sir!' Isabel exclaimed. 'You forget that Henry Viner will be sure to try and contact me, and then I shall be in even greater peril, for he will soon discover that he has been tricked.' She looked appealing at her husband. 'Indeed, I fear that man more than I can say. I beseech you, do not leave me here at his mercy.'

Sir Ralph looked thoughtful, and at last he nodded. 'Very well, madam. It shall be as you wish.' He paused. 'Will you think up some errand in the village for Alice? School her well, so that she passes on her false information in a convincing manner.'

Well primed, Alice set off and returned within the hour, pale and trembling. 'He believed me, my lady, of that I feel sure, but he wishes to meet me again tomorrow. I said I could promise nothing, because you are slightly indisposed, and I would be too busy attending you to go again to the village.'

Isabel smiled approvingly, 'Did he believe that too?'

'I think so,' Alice said. 'I was nervous, I must confess, but I covered that by allowing him to kiss me.' She shuddered. 'Oh, my lady, I long to be back in England again, but this journey terrifies me.'

They set off as arranged. A party of nine—Sir Ralph and his man, the three priests, two of Madame de Brémont's most trusted servants, one of whom was a groom, with Isabel and Alice riding in the centre of the group. At first, taking a route that avoided the village, they rode fast, but once they were well away they settled down to a steady routine, alternately trotting and walking. Stopping only for food and rest at wayside inns, and setting off early each morning, they accomplished the journey in two and a half days with no mishaps. But by the time they arrived in Boulogne, Alice was near to tears and Isabel so weary that she was nodding in the saddle.

To their great relief Sir Ralph took them to a large inn overlooking the harbour, commanded bedrooms and a private room, and left them to rest, while he went down to the quay to find a ship ready to sail the next day.

He was gone a long time. Although Isabel was so tired, she could not sleep, and eventually went to the window and stood watching the busy scene below. Suddenly a group of sailors drew apart to allow two gentlemen to pass, and her heart leapt as she saw Sir Ralph accompanied by a man whose hat was pulled well down against the wind but who, nevertheless, seemed vaguely familiar. They disappeared under the eaves and she hesitated fearfully. Was this a friend, or had Sir Ralph walked into a trap? Unable to bear the suspense, she went down to the private parlour, and the two men standing by the fire turned as she entered.

Sir Ralph spoke cordially. 'Here is an old friend of yours, madam. He has been travelling in Switzerland, visiting his wife's grave, and, learning that I was seeking to sail as soon as possible, he made himself known to me. Thanks to his intercession I have obtained places for our party on the vessel in which he himself will be travelling to England tomorrow.'

With a gasp of relief, Isabel found herself staring at Anthony's father, but then, as he bowed over her hand, her fears came flooding back. She cast a terrified look at Sir Ralph, but he was still smiling easily as though unaware of the danger of introducing a Protestant into their company.

'Mistress Isabel—no, I crave your pardon—my lady—I am extremely happy to meet you again.'

Mr Norton was looking at her closely, and as she gazed into his steady, kindly eyes, she was suddenly overwhelmed by memories of the past. Her lips trembled as he added compassionately, 'It is a shock for you to see me, but do not weep for what is gone. It was God's will.' He turned to Sir Ralph, 'I wish you both great happiness in your life together and, as we are to be travelling companions, I shall enjoy the voyage the more.'

'You will join us for supper, sir?' Sir Ralph asked, and when Mr Norton thanked him, he added easily, 'We have, as I told you, three guests who are visiting England. Ah!' He turned as the door opened. 'Here they are. Let me present them to you.'

Marvelling at his audacity, Isabel watched as Mr Norton spoke with each of the priests. Then, as they seated themselves at table, she noticed him studying them reflectively. To distract him, she asked for news of her parents.

He looked at her steadily for a moment. 'They were in good health when I last saw them, but things are not easy for Catholics now. I myself deplore intolerance, having in my youth suffered for being a Protestant. Men should be allowed to worship as they choose but, so far as I can see, the future looks black for my Catholic friends.' He gazed round the company, and continued, 'You gentlemen will have to walk very warily indeed.'

There was no mistaking the warning in his voice, and Isabel shivered inwardly. Plainly Mr Norton had a very shrewd idea that Sir Ralph's guests were seminary priests in disguise, although she felt sure that he would not betray them. Nevertheless, it would not be right to involve her kind old friend in danger and if, by some terrible misfortune, the priests should be unmasked on landing in England, Mr Norton might well be suspected of aiding and abetting their illegal entry.

Sir Ralph, however, seemed to suffer no such qualms. 'I thank you for your good advice, sir. It is a pleasure to meet a Protestant who does not uphold persecution.' He smiled. 'Let us drink a health to the day when all in England are of your opinion.'

'Amen to that,' said Mr Norton solemnly. 'Although I fear that day will be a long time coming.'

To Isabel's relief, the conversation turned to general matters, and she sat in silence until she felt she could say good night to the company and retire to her bedchamber.

Alone with Alice, she was startled when, a short time later, Sir Ralph entered the room. The maid curtsied quickly, and Sir Ralph smiled a little at her hasty exit.

'That is a good girl you have there,' he remarked. 'But you must help her to stop fearing me. She runs like a hare whenever I appear.'

In spite of her own uneasiness, Isabel laughed and spoke without thinking, 'It is natural enough. I too am somewhat in awe of you, sir.'

His smile faded and immediately she wished she had not spoken so impulsively. She half turned away, but he put his hand gently on her shoulder and turned her towards him.

'Am I then so terrifying a husband, my lady? I was beginning to hope that my presence was no longer so disagreeable to you.'

She tried to answer him lightly, but no words would come, and as his grip tightened, her heart began to hammer wildly. Helplessly she stared at him, and the flame in the depths of his dark eyes sent a shiver of desire through her whole body.

His face changed, and he let her go so suddenly that she almost fell. 'I have your answer,' he said harshly. 'To shudder thus at my touch . . .' He turned his back and stood staring out of the window while she remained motionless, gazing miserably at his rigid figure.

At last he broke the silence and, facing her once more, said stiffly, 'I came, madam, because I wished to speak of Mr Norton. If you think I have inveigled him into travelling with us, you are mistaken. He himself suggested it, so I told him as much of the truth as I dared, hinting that our guests might not be congenial to him. He has accepted this, and I am certain that he knows full well that they are priests. He travels with us of his own desire, and I am confident that he will not betray us. He insisted that my friends made no difference to him, and told me in his careful way that he might even be of service to us.' He paused, and added more gently, 'I think he is doing this for your sake. He cannot forget that Anthony loved you and, perhaps, he blames himself for forbidding him to marry you and being inadvertently the cause of his son's death.'

'He was not to blame!' Isabel found her voice at last. 'I see now that he could never have allowed such a marriage, and as for causing Anthony's death . . .' She faltered, remembering bitterly that it was she who had told Anthony about the coming of a priest. Slowly she shook her head and added almost to herself, 'The blame lies elsewhere.'

Sir Ralph recoiled as though she had struck him, and she realised too late what her words implied.

'I—I do not mean . . .' she began, but with a quick bow he left the room.

A high wind was rattling the shutters against the windows, when after a restless night Isabel rose next morning. As she entered the private parlour, Sir Ralph was saying to Mr Norton,

'No ship will put to sea in this gale. It is blowing straight from the north.

'I fear you are right, sir. I shall go down to the harbour and speak to the captain, but I expect he will tell us to wait here patiently until the wind changes.' He looked questioningly at Sir Ralph. 'Would you and your lady care to accompany me?'

'I think not. These gentlemen and I have some business to discuss, but'—Sir Ralph glanced at Isabel—'madam, would you like to go with Mr Norton?'

She agreed eagerly and soon, wrapped in a warm hooded cloak, she took Mr Norton's arm and went down to the quayside.

The captain of the ship that plied between Boulogne and Rye was a jovial red-faced man. He shook his head gloomily when Mr Norton made his tentative enquiry. 'I shall not leave the harbour today, sir,' he said firmly. 'Tomorrow, if the gale subsides in the night, I hope to catch the tide. I would be a fool to risk a ship so full—so full, indeed, that I cannot take any more passengers. Why, only a short while ago, I had to refuse a gentleman who has urgent business in England.' He chuckled. 'He confused me at first, for I thought it was the same gentleman you brought with you yesterday. There was a strong resemblance.'

Isabel looked at him sharply. 'Did he give his name, sir?'

'Why yes, I think so, my lady . . .' The captain reflected while she waited in an agony of suspense. At last he said, 'Mr Viner—Yes, that was his name.'

Isabel stood like a stone, her face so white that Mr Norton looked at her in concern, but the captain, noticing nothing, continued, 'I told him of another ship'—he jerked his head—'a smaller one, over there, and he set off in a great hurry.' He laughed boisterously. 'It will do him no good, however, for no sensible man would sail today.'

Walking back along the quayside, Isabel turned to Mr Norton, her eyes filled with terror. 'Sir Ralph must be warned at once,' she exclaimed. Then, seeing his astonishment, she burst out, 'Oh, Mr Norton—I fear that I must tell you everything!'

He listened gravely to her hurried, almost incoherent tale, and when she came to the end of it just as they were entering the paved courtyard of the inn, he said quietly, 'My dear child—for that is what you still seem to me—do not agitate yourself. I understand the situation very well. We shall find the others, and I shall see what I can do to help you.'

For a long moment she stood still, gazing at him, her heart in her eyes. As she tried to express her gratitude, he smiled gently.

'You must not thank me. My son loved you dearly, and if I can assist you, it will be for his sake.'

Sir Ralph and his companions looked up as they entered the private room and, before Isabel could speak, her husband held out a letter. 'A messenger came from my aunt. He was mighty glad to find us here, having near killed himself in chasing after us.'

She sat down on the chair he pulled up for her, and said breathlessly, 'We have news, too. The captain told us of a gentleman—Henry Viner— seeking a ship for England.'

To her surprise, Sir Ralph said calmly, 'It confirms what my aunt has written.'

She looked at the paper in her hand. The message was brief, for Madame de Brémont had written in haste. Soon after their departure, it appeared that Joseph Durand had been surprised in Sir Ralph's bedchamber. The manservant who had discovered him had tried to hold him prisoner, but unfortunately he escaped. Apparently he had reported to his master that Sir Ralph and his guests had already left, for servants sent down to the village returned with the news that Henry Viner had left the neighbourhood and taken the road to Boulogne.

Isabel handed back the letter. 'But why Boulogne? Joseph Durand could not have told him, for he did not know we had taken this route.'

'I do not think that Henry knows we are here, but, as he prefers always to stay in the background, he would not wish to be seen when we were taken by Walsingham's men. Joseph Durand will have been given the task of informing the authorities.' Sir Ralph turned to Mr Norton, and added, 'Sir, you must by now see that you are in dangerous company. I know full well that you will not betray us, but it would, I think, be safer for you to dissociate yourself from us.'

'Mr Norton knows our secret,' Isabel said quickly. 'I have told him everything, and he has offered to help us.'

After an uneasy silence, Mr Norton said calmly, 'If you will trust me, gentlemen, I shall be happy to assist you in a small way.' His mouth twisted wryly. 'My conscience and my heart are at odds with each other, but I am no Judas. If we can sail tomorrow, as our ship is larger than the one to which our captain sent Mr Viner, we should arrive first in Rye. As soon as we land, I suggest that we separate. With your permission, Sir Ralph, I shall accompany your lady to your house in Kent, and then you will be free to go where you think best with your friends.'

'I thank you, sir. It is a good plan.' Sir Ralph glanced at the priests. 'We shall go to London, where I have friends who will see to the rest.'

In the evening the wind began to die down, and while they were at table, a lad came up from the quayside with a message from the captain. He hoped, he said, to catch the tide at noon next day, and asked them to go aboard first thing in the morning.

Upstairs in her bedchamber, Isabel and Alice were making their preparations for the journey when Sir Ralph entered, and Alice quickly withdrew.

He went over to the window and gazed out, before turning to Isabel. 'Mr Norton has offered to stay with you in Overton Place until I return, which pleases me greatly. He will help you if necessary.'

'I shall be pleased to have his company, sir.' Isabel looked puzzled. 'But why should I need help? I have but to await your return from London . . .' She stopped, the blood draining from her face. 'What do you mean, sir? Do you fear that you may not come back?'

He lifted his shoulders.

'I might be, shall we say—delayed—for a short time, if we were caught.'

'Delayed? You mean . . . ?'

He nodded easily. 'Imprisoned for a while, perhaps. I mention this only to prepare you, so that you may know what to do in the unlikely event. Put yourself in Mr Norton's charge. He will advise you for the best.'

Isabel stared at him helplessly. How could she endure it if he were caught? Her heart began to race in terror as she pictured the dangers that lay ahead. Torture to make him divulge the names of his friends—Tyburn—How could he take the risk of incurring such terrible penalties so calmly? Bereft of speech, she stood motionless as he bowed and left the room.

The crossing was uneventful. After the gale, the great waves had almost subsided, and a good breeze sped them quickly to Rye. They were in sight of the harbour when Mr Norton came up from his cabin to join the rest of the party and stood with them as they gazed at the small group of people gathered on the quayside. Suddenly he pointed ahead.

'Sir Ralph! That gentleman there—do you see him? He is the one dressed in black with two rough fellows behind him. I think he will question us—he has an air of authority. I suggest you let me claim Monsieur Roget and his companions as my friends, while you stay apart with your lady wife. I have sailed from Rye on several occasions, and am known as a learned Protestant who travels often to Geneva. I do not think they will question the fact that I bring guests home with me.'

Sir Ralph frowned. 'I cannot let you take such a risk, sir. It is my duty to . . .'

'It is not a question of duty, sir.' For once Mr Norton showed a flash of anger. 'It is the safety of your friends that is at stake. You cannot afford to be reckless.'

Sir Ralph flushed, and hesitated for a moment. 'You are right, sir. Providence has sent you to us, and I would be a fool to refuse your help.'

To Isabel, hidden in her heavy cloak, the next half-hour was like a nightmare. While their papers were being scrutinised, she glanced quickly behind her and saw to her dismay that Mr Norton was being questioned by the man in black, but her involuntary gasp of fright was swiftly stifled by Sir

Ralph's easy laugh as he took back his documents.

'How good it is to be in our own country once more, my lady,' he said loudly. 'Some English ale is what you need to bring back your strength.'

Taking her arm, he led her towards the quayside inn; then, glancing back, he said softly,

'Thank God! They are following us, so all is well.'

In the crowded inn parlour he managed a word with Mr Norton and then escorted her to an upstairs chamber. 'While you are resting, I shall watch from the window to see if Henry's ship arrives. We dare not stay to eat here, so if you can endure a short while longer, we shall set off as soon as the horses are ready. You have been very courageous, my lady. I did not wish you to endure such hardship, but there is no doubt that, by your insistence on accompanying us, you have done much to ensure the success of this enterprise. Your friendship with Mr Norton has been the means of saving us all.'

She flushed at his praise. 'But you are still in danger,' she said impulsively. 'I shall not rest until you are safely back home.'

He was going towards the window, but turned quickly and came back to her, gazing down as she lay among the pillows on the shabby bed. Hesitantly he took her hand, and she let it lie unresistingly in his.

'Isabel,' he began urgently, 'do you care—do you . . .' He suddenly bent down and gathered her into his arms. 'Oh, my sweet love—if you but knew how I long for you . . .' His voice broke and, pushing aside the bodice of her dress, he buried his face on her breast.

His strong arms held her so tightly that she could scarcely breathe, and the feel of his lips raining kisses on her bare flesh caused Isabel to arch her body towards him in a fierce desire that almost frightened her by its intensity. He lifted his head and gazed at her with an expression in his eyes that drew tears to her own. The question in those dark depths was unmistakable, and as she stared back at him, she trembled with the knowledge that, at last, her moment had come. The moment in which she could tell him that she was ready to give herself up to the burning love that engulfed her in a fire of abandonment.

Her mouth opened and she tried to speak, but no words came. Exhausted by emotion, her throat was constricted and, despairingly, she felt her tears overflow.

His face grew pale and he released her slowly until she fell back on to the bed.

'Ah, no!' The words came, and she put out her arms pleadingly, but suddenly a loud knocking sounded on the door and she knew it was too late.

For a moment longer he stared down at her, then turned sharply and opened the door.

She heard a boy's voice—'The horses are ready, sir'—and then, as the lad went clattering down the stairs, Sir Ralph came to help her to rise from the bed.

'We must away,' he said. 'I wish . . . But we cannot talk now. Mr Norton will follow us.'

They came together at an inn some distance from Rye, where they ate a hasty meal, and after that there was no time for more than a quick farewell and Mr Norton led his party towards Overton Place.

*   *   *

Two days later, sitting with Mr Norton in the winter parlour, Isabel listened as he outlined his plans for his future life. He was going to sell his estate in Sussex and settle in Geneva. Vale Court, he said, held too many sad memories for him.

Isabel nodded slowly and gazed into the fire. What, she wondered sadly, did the future hold? Sir Ralph, no doubt, would continue his work of helping seminary priests, and she would have to learn to endure weeks of agonising fear whenever he undertook his perilous journeys.

Suddenly, as though in answer to her rising apprehension, there was a sound of doors slamming, raised voices and, a few moments later, the Steward entered, his usually impassive face white with shock.

'My lady—Mr Norton. A messenger has come with bad news. Sir Ralph . . .' His voice broke and he flung up his arms in a gesture of despair. 'Sir Ralph has been arrested and taken to the Tower!'

CHAPTER
THIRTEEN

ISABEL GASPED and shrank back in her chair, and Mr
Norton got quickly to his feet.

'Shut the door, Mr Fuller,' he said quietly. 'I fear
your news has shocked my lady. Will you please
pour wine?'

Remorsefully, the Steward said, 'I should not
have told you so abruptly, my lady.' The glass
shook as he handed it to her, and then he turned to
Mr Norton. 'William Holden has ridden all night
from Sir Ralph's house in London. He has told me
all that happened.' He hesitated, glancing a little
doubtfully at Mr Norton.

'There is naught to fear from me, good Mr
Fuller,' said Mr Norton calmly. 'My lady will assure
you that I, as an old friend, am to be trusted.' He
smiled reassuringly. 'I know everything, having
travelled with Sir Ralph and the three gentlemen.
Were they also taken prisoner?'

'No, sir. My master had already, thank God,
taken them to a friend's house. Then he went on to
the Strand, and had been there but a short time
when poursuivants arrived with a warrant to
search. They told him they had been given information that he was sheltering newly-arrived priests
from France. To their fury they found that he was
alone, but that did not save him, for they arrested

him. He is accused of helping Jesuits to enter this country.'

He went to take Isabel's glass. Her colour had returned, but there was anguish in her eyes as she gazed up at the two men. Her mind was filled with a vision of a dank cell in the Tower and the horrors that awaited its occupant.

'Oh, God!' she cried. 'I cannot bear it! They will torture him!'

Mr Norton bent down and put his arms gently round Isabel's shoulders, while the Steward quickly poured the wine. When she had taken a few sips, he said,

'My lady—Isabel, my child, do not sink into despair. There is much that can be done. I myself . . .' He stopped and pondered for a minute, then turned to the Steward. 'I am sure that Sir Ralph must often have envisaged the possibility of being captured. What instructions has he given you?'

'Well, sir,' Mr Fuller said, 'before he was married, I was told to warn his friends immediately, then keep his household in good order and to admit only those who had legal rights. But, for this last journey, he told me that my lady would be in France, and that I was to write and ask her to remain there either until he was released, or . . .' He stopped abruptly and Mr Norton nodded quickly.

'I understand. He had not expected his lady to accompany him. Well, she is here now, and in my charge. Perhaps it would be wise if . . .' He glanced at Isabel. 'My lady, would you not care to go to your parents' home and wait there?'

'No, sir,' Isabel replied violently. 'Much as I would like to, I cannot leave here. I must be as near to my husband as possible.' A sudden thought struck her, and she sat erect. 'I shall go to the London house, and perhaps from there I might be able to visit Sir Ralph.'

Mr Norton thought for a moment. 'Yes, I do not think you will be in any danger, and I shall try to obtain permission for you.' He turned again to the Steward. 'Mr Fuller, these friends of Sir Ralph's— Is it possible that they might help him in some way or other?'

'No, sir, I fear not,' the Steward said sadly. 'My orders were to warn them, but Sir Ralph also said that on no account were they to betray themselves by coming forward to intercede for him. Those were my instructions, and I dare not go against them. There is too much at stake.'

'Very well,' Mr Norton said. 'Now let us have the messenger up here. He may have more to tell us.'

Still wearing his travel-stained riding-clothes, William Holden came into the room. Even in her grief Isabel could see that the man had aged visibly. The sturdy cheerful servant who had helped to smooth the way on that difficult journey through France had changed into a grim-faced man full of subdued fury that he had not been able to save his master.

Sir Ralph, he told them, had not resisted arrest, but he had delayed the poursuivants in every manner possible in order to enable the servant to slip away and warn Gilbert White and the priests who were with him in Chancery Lane. By the time William had returned to the Strand, Sir Ralph had been taken to the Tower and the house closed and guarded.

'Do you think, sir,' he looked anxiously at Mr

Norton, 'that I would be allowed into the Tower? I could take some necessities to Sir Ralph and give him messages from my lady and you.'

Mr Norton replied sorrowfuly. 'No, William. I do not think such privileges will be allowed. Sir Francis Walsingham's prisoners are not treated as honourable gentlemen. Our only hope is that the Queen, when hearing of Sir Ralph's arrest, may remember that she owes a debt of gratitude to him and his family. She has never yet forgotten those who befriended her in her own distress. I must find a suitable person to plead his cause.'

'I shall go . . .' Isabel exclaimed. 'I shall beg her on my knees!'

'No, my lady,' Mr Norton said gravely. 'You have never been to Court, and you are young and beautiful. Her Grace . . .' He added dryly, 'The Queen has no great liking for her own sex.' He turned to William. 'What did they say in Chancery Lane when you told them of Sir Ralph's arrest?'

'There were several gentlemen there, sir, and as soon as they heard my news, Mr White sent the three priests on their journey. They were bound for the North Country. Then Mr White asked me many questions. I told him . . .' He went on awkwardly. 'I told him of you, sir. That you were a Protestant gentleman who had helped us to land by satisfying the questioners at Rye. He sent his heartfelt thanks.'

There was a long silence, then William, with a quick compassionate glance at Isabel, went on, 'Mr White said that the fact that the three priests had escaped would no doubt anger Sir Francis Walsingham so much that, although nothing could be proved against Sir Ralph, he might yet try to make him talk.' He stopped as Isabel gasped in horror, then continued hurriedly. 'Mr White said he thought the Queen would not approve, and therefore Sir Francis might not tell her until he had had his way with Sir Ralph.'

'So it would seem that Her Grace had best be informed as soon as possible,' said Mr Fuller gravely. 'Well, thank you, William, you have done well.'

The servant bowed and left them, and Isabel, her mind in a turmoil of fear, looked at Mr Norton, who was deep in thought. Suddenly he clasped his hands together and exclaimed,

'I have it! The Bishop of London is our man! John Aylmer is an old friend. I knew him when my wife and I were in exile during Queen Mary's reign. He came back from Switzerland with me when Queen Elizabeth succeeded to the throne.' He gave a grimace. 'I have played many a game of bowls with him and, as he always likes to win and I am no expert, we remain on good terms.'

'A Protestant Bishop?' Isabel stared at Mr Norton incredulously. 'Why should he do aught for a Catholic?'

Mr Norton smiled a little sardonically. 'Bishop Aylmer is not in favour of recusants being imprisoned. He considers that fines are preferable and a good way of filling the Queen's coffers. Sir Ralph may have to pay heavily for his release. It will be difficult, for he is accused of more than recusancy. He is under well-founded suspicion that he helps seminary priests to enter England. But Sir Ralph is very rich, and in the Bishop's eyes that may tip the balance. John Aylmer is a fiery man, very hot against the Catholics, but he dislikes Puritans almost as much and is no friend of Sir Francis Walsingham, the most fanatical Puritan of them all. Her Grace, though she gives great power to Sir Francis, takes after her Royal father in loving wealth and possessions and will, I hope, incline to the Bishop's view, especially as Sir Ralph's father once befriended her.'

There was a long silence as Isabel pondered his words, and then Mr Norton rose and bowed.

'There is no time to be lost. I shall go immediately to seek an interview with John Aylmer. I should be there tomorrow.'

He turned at the door as a thought struck him. 'My lady, I think perhaps it would be a good thing for you to come with me to London. Mr Fuller here and William, along with your maid, could accompany you.'

'But there will be watchers placed outside the house, sir. Do you think they will allow me to enter?'

'I think they cannot stop Sir Ralph's wife from entering her own house, my lady. You are not under suspicion,' said Mr Norton calmly. 'If you wish, I shall accompany you there myself, and then go to the Governor of the Tower to try to obtain an order for you to visit your husband.'

They set out for London within the hour, but when at last they reached Sir Ralph's house in the Strand, Isabel's spirits sank at the sight of the guard outside the great doors. Mr Norton, however, spoke quietly to him, and after a few minutes' consultation he stood aside.

It was plain to see that Sir Ralph's arrest had cast the household into disarray and that the search had been conducted with scant respect for the furnishings. The servants had done their best to restore order, but there was an air of desolation everywhere, with tapestries torn down and panelling pierced, pictures thrown aside and floorboards wrenched up. Isabel was thankful when the Steward took command, and eventually they sat down to a hurriedly prepared meal.

Mr Norton had left the house when Isabel descended the stairs next morning. In order to keep herself from dwelling on the fears that threatened to overwhelm her, she went on an inspection of the house. But in spite of the splendid furnishings and all the evidence of great wealth, she drew no comfort from her surroundings. What did it matter to her that she was mistress of all this grandeur when Sir Ralph was lying in prison with a dreadful fate hanging over him? Without him to share her life, all would be dust and ashes.

At last, after hours of waiting during which her nerves were stretched nearly to breaking-point, Mr Norton returned. At his request, Isabel summoned Mr Fuller to hear his news, and they drank wine while Mr Norton unfolded his story.

'I was fortunate in that, as soon as I sent in my name, the Bishop consented to see me, but when I asked him to plead for Sir Ralph, he grew exceedingly angry, and anger from John Aylmer is a very noisy affair.' He smiled wryly. 'He reproached me bitterly for taking the part of a recusant and traitor, and said that if I persisted in meddling in such affairs I would find myself in danger from Walsingham and his spies.'

For a few moments Mr Norton sipped his wine reflectively. Then, seeing the dismay on Isabel's

face, he hastened to console her. 'That was his first
reaction, but when at last he paused to draw breath,
I begged him to bear with me, for there was much to
tell. I went back into the past and told him how
Anthony, my son, had died and how I blamed
myself for his death. He shook his head at that and
said that no good Protestant parent could have
allowed such a marriage, but my distress softened
his heart, for he listened attentively to the rest of
my story. On hearing that Sir Ralph's father had
helped the Queen when she was herself a prisoner,
his manner changed. Her Grace, he said, would be
exceeding wrathful if she knew that Sir Ralph had
been imprisoned without her knowledge or consent. He grew very thoughtful, and at last he said,
almost gleefully—for he has no liking for the man—
that Walsingham had gone too far this time.' Mr
Norton picked up his glass again and smiled triumphantly, 'The upshot of it was that John
Aylmer, Bishop of London, promised to seek an
audition with the Queen to plead for Sir Ralph's
release.'

Isabel clasped her hands to her breast, and Mr
Fuller exclaimed,

'Thank God! And thank you, sir, for all you have
done.'

Mr Norton put up his hand. 'Ah! But we must not
be too confident. We must wait patiently for at least
three days, for John Aylmer said he could not hope
to see the Queen before that.' He turned to Isabel.
'Unfortunately, my lady, I have failed to obtain
permission for you to visit your husband. The
Lieutenant at the Tower would not allow it, as Sir
Ralph has not yet been questioned.'

'Questioned?' The word spelt horror to Isabel.

'You mean . . .' She stopped, as a dreadful vision of the rack sprang instantly to her mind.

'No, no,' Mr Norton said hastily. 'There will be time for the Bishop to see Her Grace before they do their worst.'

It seemed to Isabel that the waiting time would never pass. She withdrew to her bedchamber where, in between her desperate prayers for Sir Ralph, she wept for her own coldness towards him. Beginning to fear that the Bishop's plea would be disregarded, she tried to think of a plan whereby, if all else failed, she herself could help to obtain his release. Her thoughts grew wilder and more and more impossible, until at last she gave up and became so listless that Alice, in alarm, went in search of Mr Norton.

He went straight to her room and stood looking down at her sternly. 'My lady, you will not help your husband by giving way to despair. It is a bright day, though cold, so wrap yourself warmly and come with me. I shall show you something of London.'

She shook her head, but he persisted, and seeing the disappointment in his kind eyes, a wave of shame swept over her. She rose and took his hand. 'I shall take courage from your strength, sir. You are so good to me, and it is not fit that I should seem ungrateful.'

Soon, walking beside him, they went outside and Mr Norton exchanged a few words with the guard, who shrugged his shoulders and nodded uninterestedly. But there was something alarming about the insolent way in which he stared at Isabel, and she would have fled back inside but for Mr Norton's restraining arm.

Gradually, however, she began to take an interest in her surroundings and, country girl that she was, found the noise and activity almost overwhelming. The narrow streets, the apprentices extolling their masters' wares, the stalls ranged along the pathways, all the bargaining and shouting coming from what seemed to her to be countless hundreds of moving indifferent folk, was frightening yet stimulating. Ragged children dodged among the horses and carts, beggars cried out for alms, and street-criers offered everything from hot mutton pies to fresh herrings. The discordant hubbub nearly deafened her. She glanced up at the endless roofs and the houses with their leaning windows, and stared at personages of interest that her companion pointed out. Sober city merchants wearing rich gold chains and long fur-trimmed robes passed by in earnest discussion, groups of gallants swaggered along, their magnificent costumes contrasting sharply with those of the ministers in black gowns and white ruffs—they mingled in a riot of colour that left her dazed and breathless.

At last Mr Norton pointed ahead. 'The Tower.'

Isabel gripped his arm convulsively, and quickened her flagging steps. 'Let us go nearer. Do you know where Sir Ralph is lodged?'

'No, but I do not think he will be too badly housed for the first few days,' he said, though privately he considered that any of those evil-smelling cells would be hard to endure. He glanced at her compassionately. 'When you have looked your fill, we shall go back by water, for you must be weary.'

Isabel thanked him abstractedly, her eyes fixed on the grey towers, the high keep and the battlemented walls of the great fortress brooding over the City like some monstrous beast. How much misery, she wondered, was enclosed within those thick walls? Suddenly she turned away.

'I can bear no more,' she said brokenly. 'Let us go back.'

Walking slowly down to the river, she was silent and withdrawn until Mr Norton startled her by stopping so abruptly that she fell against him.

'That gentleman paying off a boatman—look ahead—do you see him?'

She followed his gaze and then shrank back. 'Henry Viner!' she exclaimed and shuddered violently. 'Oh, God! Can we not avoid him?'

'It is too late,' Mr Norton murmured. 'Pull your hood well up and look towards the ground.'

Mr Viner seemed in a great hurry, and made no sign of recognition as he strode up the slope, but a minute after he had passed, Isabel glanced back and saw him standing still, staring after them.

'Come quickly,' said Mr Norton. 'The wherry is waiting. Mr Viner will not follow us. Dismiss him from your mind, my lady. His task is accomplished. He can do you no more harm.'

That night, weary from her long walk, Isabel slept well, and the next morning Mr Norton came to her holding a letter in his hand.

'I am summoned to the Bishop,' he announced jubilantly. 'He has seen Her Grace, who gave him a great roasting for his audacity, but finally allowed herself to be persuaded. Sir Ralph is to be freed.' He paused and handed her the letter. 'There are certain conditions, and those I shall be told when I receive the order of release which he says I myself may take to the Tower.'

She looked apprehensive. 'Conditions? Do you think Sir Ralph will accept them? If they mean that he must abjure his religion, it will all be in vain.'

'No,' Mr Norton said reassuringly. 'You need have no fear on that score. I explained to John Aylmer what manner of man Sir Ralph is. It will be, I fear, a great fine, but Sir Ralph will be well able to fulfil that condition.' He bowed. 'My lady, I must be on my way if he is to return home today.'

Once more Isabel waited, but this time hope filled her heart to such an extent that the passing hours seemed interminable. In the afternoon she began to feel uneasy, and in order to keep calm she went to her bedchamber and lay down on the bed. Suddenly she lifted her head at the sound she had been waiting for so impatiently. Voices down below at last. She jumped from the bed and stood rigidly watching the door, unable to move, her nerves tense with joyful anticipation.

Then, with a crash, it was flung open and for one brief moment her heart leapt.

'Ralph!' She ran forward but then stopped and would have fallen had Henry Viner not gripped her arm.

'Sit down, my lady,' he said softly. 'You had best collect your wits, for you have much explaining to do.'

He turned quickly as a shriek came from behind, and Alice ran past him to clasp Isabel protectively in her arms.

His eyes glinted with fury. 'Release your mistress, wench, and do not try to summon help. The servants have been told that I am here to assist my lady.'

He went to the door, holding it open while he

peered down the passage. Then, with a gasp of terror, Isabel heard him say,

'Come in, Joseph. Take this woman into a quiet room and tie her up. Then go down and make sure that the other servants suspect nothing. If screams should be heard, you must say that my lady is hysterical but that her maid is tending her.'

A wiry fox-like man came grinning into the room and Alice shrieked again. In a flash he had his hand over her mouth, and she was wrenched away and dragged outside.

Isabel ran forward, calling for help, but it was too late. Henry Viner slammed the door and lifted her, kicking and fighting on to the bed. With strength reinforced by wild terror, she scratched and tore at him until, viciously, he struck her hard across her mouth. She collapsed and lay still, staring up at him in frozen horror.

'Now, madam'—his face was distorted with fury—'you shall pay for daring to deceive me. Ralph is in the Tower and, I trust, will go to Tyburn. The priests, however, have escaped and, as a result, Walsingham refuses to grant me your husband's estates. For that you shall suffer dearly. If you resist me, I shall kill you at once.'

The room closed in on her, but, with a great effort, she forced herself back to consciousness just as he tore her dress from her shoulders, ripping it down the front and leaving her nearly naked. She began to shriek, but he flung himself on to her, stifling her exhausted cries. The feel of his hands gripping her breasts drove her nearly frantic, and as she was struggling wildly to rise, she saw his dagger fall on to the end of the bed. Furiously he hit her again and again until she fell sideways, half over the edge of the bed. Then, just as he began to pull her back, she reached out with one last great effort, seized the dagger, and drove it with all her waning force into his side.

"God's Death! You vixen!' He sprang to his feet, and the dagger clattered to the floor as she stood aghast, staring at the blood pouring from the wound.

She fell back on the bed for a moment, then, shaking and nauseated, she pulled her dress round her and got to her feet.

Leaning against the wall, his hands over the wound, Henry Viner's face was deathly white, and even as she watched, he slid down on to his knees.

Suddenly an icy calm took possession of her, and, opening the door, she called again and again for help. It was not until she began to walk along the passage that she heard the sound of scuffling and shouting, and at last two men-servants came rushing up the stairs.

She led them back and pointed to Henry Viner, now lying unconscious on the floor.

'Take him to another room and send his servant to tend him,' she said. They stared at her for a moment, then, as darkness began to close in on her, she gasped, 'Find Alice—she is tied up somewhere.'

She recovered consciousness to find Alice bathing her forehead and bruised face and, as her vision cleared, she gave a weak cry of joy at the sight of the tall figure standing at the foot of the bed.

With one swift step Sir Ralph came to her side and fell on his knees.

'Oh, God be thanked!' she exclaimed, and all went black again.

Later, when the room had been cleaned, she told her story to Sir Ralph and Mr Norton. It did not take long, but during those few minutes, Sir Ralph's face turned white with rage and a pulse began to beat at his temple. His eyes blazed so fiercely that Mr Norton put out a gentle hand to calm him as he began to speak.

'The wound you gave him was not deep enough. He will, I regret, recover. But I shall not see him again, for I do not trust myself not to finish him off.'

Isabel shuddered. 'I am thankful he is not dead. I could not have borne to be a murderess.'

Mr Norton shook his head. 'My child, you were defending your virtue. It would not have been a crime, even if you had killed him.'

'Did he succeed?' Sir Ralph's voice was so harsh that she shrank back.

'Succeed? I do not understand you, sir.'

'Your virtue—Did he accomplish what he set out to do?'

'Sir Ralph!' Mr Norton expostulated. 'There is no need to be so brutal. Your lady wife was helpless . . . If only I had not taken Mr Fuller with me.' He stopped as Isabel turned to look steadily at her husband.

'No, sir,' she said calmly. 'Henry Viner did not have his way. I thought I had already told you. Do you not believe me?' She added very quietly, 'And if he had succeeded, would the fault have been mine?'

'Ah, no, madam! You mistake my meaning.' Sir Ralph put his hand on hers. 'My rage is not directed at you. You have been so courageous that you make me feel unworthy. But if . . .' His eyes blazed again. 'If he had taken you, then no power on earth would stop me from finishing what you began.'

Mr Norton spoke gently. 'Your fury is natural, sir, but thank God your lady was able to protect herself. I shall leave you now, for you will have much to say to each other.' He bowed and then paused in the doorway. 'I shall go to look at Mr Viner, to make sure he has not developed a fever. Will you permit him to stay here until he has recovered?'

Sir Ralph frowned, then gave a wry smile. 'Yes, he shall have what care is necessary, but as soon as he is able I want him out of my house. His man may go with him to his lodgings or wherever he chooses. I gave him an estate in Dorset—no doubt he will take advantage of it. It is evident that Walsingham, who does not like to be foiled, will no longer have need of his services.'

There was a long silence after the door closed. Then Sir Ralph said quietly, 'Are you strong enough to hear bad news, madam?'

Isabel stared at him in astonishment mingled with alarm. 'Bad news, sir? But I thought Her Grace had pardoned you.'

'Not pardoned. Released on certain conditions, to which I had perforce to agree.' He sat scowling for several minutes, and Isabel's fears rose to such a pitch that she could bear it no longer.

'The bad news, sir. Pray, do not torment me. What are these conditions?'

He lifted his head and stared at her almost in surprise. 'Your pardon, madam. My thoughts were elsewhere,' he said slowly, and relapsed once more into silence. At last he continued.

'I had a choice. In order to be completely pardoned and to be received at Court again—even, it
was promised, to rise high in the Queen's favour—I
had to repudiate my religion publicly and become a
Protestant. That, of course, I refused to do. The
alternative was hard but acceptable.' He gazed at
her searchingly. 'You, I think, will find it more
painful than I do, for I know you hold wealth and
possessions in high esteem.'

She opened her mouth to speak, but he went on
resolutely.

'I am to be banished from the realm, madam, and
my estates made forfeit to the Crown. I have a
month in which to put my affairs in order, and if I
am found in this land one day after that time, I shall
be imprisoned as before, with no hope of release.'

Stricken with grief and unable to find words to
comfort him, Isabel closed her eyes, while tears
trickled down her white face. Banishment from all
that he loved: his country, his estates, the beautiful
house in Kent which had been in his family for
generations, and condemned to be an exile in a
foreign land for the rest of his days. She gave a great
sob, and opened her eyes to see him gazing at her
with a sorrowful look that went straight to her
heart.

Then he said harshly, 'I understand your grief,
madam. You will no longer be the wife of a wealthy
husband, and no doubt you will choose to return to
your parents—which I give you full leave to do. Do
not fear that you will be destitute, however, for I
made over a large sum to be paid to you in the event
of my being punished for my activities. Those
monies cannot be taken from you so long as you
remain in this country.' He stopped for a moment,

glanced quickly at her stricken face, then added, 'Perhaps, as your religious convictions are not very strong, you could petition for an annulment. Although I would never consider myself free to marry again, nor would I wish to, it might be easier for you to plan your future.'

Stunned by the realisation that, even now, Sir Ralph did not understand that she loved him, Isabel was speechless. At last, slowly, she turned her face towards him. 'Why may not I share your exile, sir? Surely a wife's place is at her husband's side? Or do you wish to be quit of me, finding that I am tiresome and difficult?'

'Quit of you? God's Body!' His eyes flamed. 'You know, or should know, that I love you as my life's blood. But you yourself admitted that you married me because I was rich. Now, since by my own fault I have forfeited all that held you to me, you have the right to consider yourself deceived in your expectations.'

Overcome by his vehemence, she turned her head away again, but her heart seemed as though it would burst with joy.

'You cannot face me, madam, for you know that what I say is true,' Sir Ralph said bitterly. 'Although I shall always love you, I do not wish you to accompany me into exile from a sense of duty.' He then said quietly, as though to himself, 'You were frank with me when you said you would never love anyone but Anthony. I was a fool to think that, one day, you might come to care for me.'

Isabel drew a sigh of pure happiness. 'But I do love you, sir.'

He rose abruptly and stood staring down at her incredulously.

'God's Life! What did you say?'

She tried to speak, but her heart was beating so rapidly that she felt as though she would die of joy in this sweet moment of surrender. Then she saw that he was trembling in an agony of suspense, and she found her voice.

'I loved Anthony as a young girl loves a boy. But I am a woman now, and my love for you'—She hesitated as her pale face suddenly flooded with colour—'Well, it is of a different kind. Wealth and possessions no longer have any meaning for me. To be with you will be riches indeed.' Her voice broke on a sob, and she put her arms out pleadingly, 'I shall die, I think, if you do not take me with you.'

'Dear Mother of God!' said Sir Ralph softly, and suddenly he was on his knees beside her, his arms clasping her tightly, his head on her breast.

Mills & Boon

Your chance to step into the past Take 2 Books FREE

Discover a world long vanished. An age of chivalry and intrigue, powerful desires and exotic locations. Read about true love found by soldiers and statesmen, princesses and serving girls. All written as only Mills & Boon's top-selling authors know how. Become a regular reader of Mills & Boon Masquerade Historical Romances and enjoy 4 superb, new titles every two months, plus a whole range of special benefits: your very own personal membership card entitles you to a regular free newsletter packed with recipes, competitions, exclusive book offers plus other bargain offers and big cash savings.

AND an Introductory FREE GIFT for YOU.
Turn over the page for details.

**Fill in and send this coupon back today
and we will send you**

2 Introductory
Historical Romances
FREE

At the same time we will reserve a subscription to
Mills & Boon Masquerade Historical Romances for
you. Every two months you will receive Four new,
superb titles delivered direct to your door. You
don't pay extra for delivery. Postage and packing is
always completely free. There is no obligation or
commitment – you only receive books for as long as
you want to.

**Just fill in and post the coupon today to MILLS & BOON
READER SERVICE, FREEPOST, P.O. BOX 236, CROYDON,
SURREY CR9 9EL.**

**Please Note:- READERS IN SOUTH AFRICA write to
Mills & Boon, Postbag X3010,
Randburg 2125, S. Africa.**

FREE BOOKS CERTIFICATE

**To: Mills & Boon Reader Service, FREEPOST, P.O. Box 236,
Croydon, Surrey CR9 9EL.**

Please send me, free and without obligation, two Masquerade Historical Romances, and
reserve a Reader Service Subscription for me. If I decide to subscribe I shall receive,
following my free parcel of books, four new Masquerade Historical Romances every two
months for £5.00, post and packing free. If I decide not to subscribe, I shall write to you
within 10 days. The free books are mine to keep in any case. I understand that I may cancel
my subscription at any time simply by writing to you. I am over 18 years of age.

Please write in BLOCK CAPITALS.

Signature _____

Name _____

Address _____

_____ Post code _____

SEND NO MONEY — TAKE NO RISKS.

Please don't forget to include your Postcode.

Remember, postcodes speed delivery. Offer applies in UK only and is not valid
to present subscribers. Mills & Boon reserve the right to exercise discretion in
granting membership. If price changes are necessary you will be notified.

4M Offer expires June 30th 1985.

EP9M